A Tail of Love

A Tail of Love

Alice Sharpe

THORNDIKE
CHIVERS

This Large Print edition is published by Thorndike Press, Waterville, Maine, USA and by BBC Audiobooks Ltd, Bath, England.
Thorndike Press is an imprint of Thomson Gale, a part of The Thomson Corporation.
Thorndike is a trademark and used herein under license.

All characters in this book have no existence outside the imagination of the author and have no relation whatsoever to anyone bearing the same name or names. They are not even distantly inspired by any individual known or unknown to the author, and all the incidents are pure invention.

The text of this Large Print edition is unabridged.
Other aspects of the book may vary from the original edition.
Set in 16 pt. Plantin.

LIBRARY OF CONGRESS CATALOGING-IN-PUBLICATION DATA

Sharpe, Alice.
A tail of love : perpetually yours / by Alice Sharpe.
p. cm. — (Thorndike Press large print romance)
ISBN-13: 978-0-7862-9462-6 (lg. print : alk. paper)
ISBN-10: 0-7862-9462-0 (lg. print : alk. paper)
1. Large type books. I. Title.
PS3569.H34358T35 2007
813'.54—dc22 2007004536

BRITISH LIBRARY CATALOGUING-IN-PUBLICATION DATA AVAILABLE

Published in 2007 in the U.S. by arrangement with Harlequin Books S.A.
Published in 2007 in the U.K. by arrangement with Harlequin Enterprises II B.V.

U.K. Hardcover: 978 1 405 64086 2 (Chivers Large Print)
U.K. Softcover: 978 1 405 64087 9 (Camden Large Print)

Printed in the United States of America on permanent paper
10 9 8 7 6 5 4 3 2 1

This book is dedicated to the real Marnie
and her loving companions, my mother
and father, Mary and Philip LeVelle.

Dear Reader,

When I first thought of writing a book featuring a dog as a viewpoint character, I naturally thought of my yellow Lab, Annie Rose. But as the plot developed, it became clear I needed a protagonist with better manipulative tendencies (Annie is too anxious to please!) and at that point, my parents' little wire fox terrier came to mind.

And why not? Bouncy, determined, feisty, single-minded, their little Marnie had every quality a true heroine must possess. It's been a great deal of fun trying to think like Marnie might think, to see life from her vantage point. As much as I enjoyed writing this story, I hope you enjoy *my* Marnie's attempts to put right a love affair gone wrong, to make sure that in the end, it's happily ever after for everyone — especially Marnie!

Alice Sharpe

Chapter One

I'm a patient dog.

Okay, okay, I'm not patient, but on this particular day, I was acting patient.

Well, for a wire fox terrier, anyway.

Plastered as I was to our hostess's front door, I indulged myself with just the occasional yip to remind Isabelle it was closing in on my dinner hour. It didn't seem to be working, mainly because her girlfriend, Heather, was noisily boo-hooing in her ear.

A thump out in the hallway provided some much needed distraction, and I reacted with my usual quick wit. There is no better way to warn away ne'er-do-wells than to bark. Ask anyone.

This got Isabelle's attention. As she ordered me to mind my manners, her distraught friend jumped to her feet, almost tripping over me in her haste to pull open the door.

I'm not sure who or what she expected to find out there, but surely it wasn't the startled kid I saw. Figuring he was up to no good, I did Heather a favor and bounded after him. Isabelle ended my pursuit with a yank on my leash — which, by the way, smarts — so I trotted back to her side. No matter, the boy had left, my job was done.

Isabelle called me a bad dog, which she does often but never with much conviction, so I took it as I usually do.

That's when I noticed the folded newspaper that had magically appeared on the carpet right outside Heather's door. Looking up and down the hall, I saw a few more placed in front of other doors. Curious, no?

Ready to parlay the open door into actual leave-taking, I strained on my leash a bit. Ignoring me, Isabelle gently rolled the newspaper inside with the toe of her shoe and then closed the door. Heather launched into a new round of caterwauling. My stomach growled.

After five minutes, I tried a demure woof. After another couple of minutes, I laid down and stared at the newspaper. It was wrapped with a bright blue rubber band. Interesting. I gave it a nip, but they don't make rubber bands like they used to and the thing snapped. The paper sprang open.

And that's when I saw him.

Right there in the margin above the headline. Three pictures. One of a gooey piece of pie — looked tasty — another of some guy shooting a basketball and the last one of Rick, smiling.

My Rick.

What was his mug doing in the newspaper?

This was one of those occasions when I wished I'd learned to read, but Isabelle gets all her news off her computer and the screen is way too high off the floor to be dog-friendly. I tried tugging on the leash. Figuring there might be another picture of Rick hidden inside the newsprint, I clawed at the paper.

You have to understand. Seeing Rick at this particular juncture had to be fate. I'd been dreaming about him lately. We'd be on the beach, roasting hot dogs. He'd throw a stick, I'd run the other way, he'd dash after me, I'd run the other way — good, dog-worthy dreams of fresh air and yummy snacks.

Since he'd walked out on me and Isabelle four years before, I'd had to settle for dreams. I missed Rick. Some of the guys Isabelle brought around were okay, but one or two hadn't liked dogs. Of course, they didn't tell Isabelle this. I just knew. A dog always does.

Anyway, lately I'd been thinking it was time for Isabelle and Rick to get back together. I was tired of being the victim of a broken relationship.

And now this.

Unfortunately, newsprint isn't the most resilient of materials; within a few seconds, the thing began to shred. At least that got Isabelle's attention. She scooped up the tattered heap and handed it to Heather without so much as glancing at the front page.

Rats.

I wanted her to see that photograph of Rick. I wanted her to remember him. It had been ages since she'd spoken his name. Concentrating real hard on Rick's face, I willed her to look at the paper. I willed him, wherever he was, to think about us.

Before I knew what was happening, the two women were hugging goodbye and Isabelle and I were headed down the hall toward the elevator.

This meant we were on our way home.

Kibble!

Feeling peckish, I walked extra fast. But that's not to say I wasn't still pondering what Rick had done to get his picture in the paper.

Or why he'd left us in the first place. . . .

With a sigh, Isabelle Winters pushed the Down button. What an ordeal the afternoon had been.

Heather's husband had walked out on her. He claimed he needed space. That phrase always made Isabelle feel like scratching her head. What space? Where did this "space" exist? In some alternate universe? What did you do when you got there? Did you sit down and contemplate your navel or stumble about, anxious should you bump into someone else's "space"?

There were two twists on Heather's predicament. The least important was the fate of Heather's small catering business. How could she manage her upcoming commitments without John's help? The more serious by far was that John didn't know Heather was pregnant and Heather didn't know if she should tell him. How could she get him back if she didn't? If she did tell him and he did come back, how would she know it was for the right reasons?

Three hours of this circular logic had Isabelle's head aching. She'd murmured a few words of comfort and thrown in her two cents *(Forget the business for now! Call him! Tell him about the baby!)*, but what else could she do?

Pawing at the carpet in front of the elevator, Marnie made little anxious sounds. The doors swished open and Marnie all but dragged Isabelle inside.

"You were not a good dog," Isabelle said, as she punched the Lobby button. Looking down at her dog's upturned face, she added,

"I don't know what got into you. All that racket. And destroying Heather's newspaper!"

Marnie blinked.

The elevator soon delivered them to the lobby. Marnie pranced at the end of her leash, seventeen pounds of wire hair terrier covered with crisp white, black-and-tan fur, tawny ears bobbing, black nose sniffing, dog tags jingling, dark eyes taking in the posh lobby of Heather's apartment building.

One of the things Isabelle admired about her dog was her endless enthusiasm. Another was her take-no-prisoners approach to life. What she liked least, however, was Marnie's absolute remorselessness. However, since scolding her was pointless, holding a grudge seemed pointless, too.

Isabelle became aware of a man pushing open the outside door to enter the glass-enclosed vestibule separating the lobby from the outside. He turned immediately to face the intercom.

As Isabelle pulled the door open for him, all hell broke loose. Marnie, a blur of tri-colored fur, lunged, wiggled and bounced as she circled the man again and again, wrapping his legs in her leash, yapping and squealing the whole time. Despite Isabelle's best efforts, the stranger was soon trussed up like a calf at a rodeo.

Unnerved by Marnie's high-decibel yelps and the deep sounds coming from the startled man's throat, Isabelle murmured both apologies and reprimands as she struggled with the leash.

She finally dared a glance at the man's face. For a second her brain refused to accept what her eyes told her.

How could this be?

"Rick?"

"Isabelle! I didn't know you lived here!"

"I don't. Do you?"

"No, I'm visiting a . . . friend," he said. "And you?"

"I'm visiting a friend, too."

Marnie, bound to Rick's legs and perched more or less on his shoes, leaked delighted squeaks. He bent to pat her head and tousle her V-shaped ears. Staring right into her beady little eyes, he crooned, "Hey there, lamb chop, long time no see. How are you?" With a swift glance up at Isabelle, he added, "I see my girl is still . . . excitable."

"It was almost like she was expecting you," Isabelle added, a catch in her throat. Lamb chop! The long-forgotten puppy name brought back a host of memories, all of them bittersweet.

She undid Marnie's lead so Rick could

unbind himself. When he gave her back the leash, their fingers brushed.

"Sorry," she said.

He smiled, and it was suddenly hard to believe more than four years had passed since they'd parted ways.

Of course, when they'd been . . . together . . . he'd been in graduate school, on the fast track, but still a student. He'd worn his dark hair long, walked around in jeans and sweaters, and slouched his six-foot-four-inch frame down a notch or two to blend in. She'd been a few years younger and still an undergrad, a good deal shorter, but wore her dark hair about the same way he did and dressed in a similar fashion. They'd looked like a couple even before they became one.

Now he was Mr. Suave, hair professionally cut, wearing an expensive raincoat over an even more expensive suit. Add Italian shoes and perfect posture and he looked like what he'd become — the youngest member in Portland, Oregon's, most prestigious law firm.

And so handsome there ought to be a law.

"You look wonderful," he said, raking her over with a gaze that used to make her shiver. Thinking of her hair caught up in a ponytail and the jeans and sweatshirt she'd thrown on in haste when Heather beckoned her to Portland, Isabelle mumbled a thanks.

"How is your family?" he asked politely. "Your father retired yet? Your mother still golfing twice a day?"

"Dad's still working, Mom's still golfing," Isabelle said fondly. "I took a job in Seaport about two years ago now."

He nodded thoughtfully, and she wondered if it was because of all the memories they shared of the town in which she now lived or because his estranged father also lived and worked there. She decided not to mention that she saw his father often, that they'd remained friends, that Rick's absence in both their lives had taken a long time to heal.

Rick said, "I thought I heard somewhere that you're teaching kindergarten."

"I have twenty-three kids," she said. "There's only a few more days of school until summer vacation, so of course they're all getting a little wild."

She stopped abruptly, right as she'd been about to launch into an anecdote about one of her students. Why would big-time lawyer Rick want to hear about someone else's kid?

"It's what you always wanted," he said. "I'm proud of you for pursuing your dream."

Rick hadn't pursued his dream. He'd chased money instead. And in so doing, he'd abandoned her. That's how she felt, that's how she'd always felt. She tried hard not to show it because it was water under the bridge.

"It's actually rather fortuitous I ran into you," he said.

She did not feel fortunate in any way. For four years, she'd put Rick behind her to the point that when she saw his father now, she didn't even think about Rick.

Liar, came an internal voice. *You never put him behind you.*

"I did, too!" she said.

Rick had been talking, but he stopped abruptly. She'd spoken out loud. She knew her comment made no sense. More than anything in the world, she wanted to escape this tiny foyer.

She said, "It's been a very long day, Rick."

"Wait," he said, briefly touching her arm. "I want to hear about your classroom —"

"No you don't," she said, meeting his gaze. "They're just a bunch of little five-year-olds. They wouldn't interest you."

"I see," he said, his dark eyes flashing. "I'm too busy raking in the corporate dough to care about a bunch of little kids, is that it?"

Things were going from bad to worse, but damn, he was making her angry. Pitching a little more fuel on the fire, she added, "Or maybe you spend your time figuring out ways to keep the bad guys out of jail."

He seemed to swallow a retort. Glancing at his watch, he said, "I'd better go."

She'd been rude. She couldn't seem to think of a way to apologize without making it worse. What did it matter anyway? It had been years since she'd seen him, it would probably be years more before she saw him again. If ever . . .

She said, "I have to go, too."

They stared at each other for a moment, then Rick grasped her elbow, and leaning close, kissed her cheek. The closeness of his strong body and the feel of his lips on her face evoked still more memories.

"It was great seeing you again," he said.

"You, too," she told him, but she didn't mean it. Seeing him had been painful. She felt rattled and slightly nauseous.

And contrite. She put her arm around his neck and hugged him. He felt solid and real in a way only an old love can feel: at once familiar and yet foreign. She let go of him and backed toward the outside door.

Kneeling, Rick ruffled Marnie who gazed at him with unaffected adoration, an expression for which her breed was not famous. "You be a good dog," he told her. Then he whispered something else close to her ear and accepted a quick lick of his cheek before standing again.

The innocent little beast panted with joy, not realizing that Rick's words meant so-long, goodbye, take care, see you . . . never again.

Raindrops pelted the windshield. Oregon was having a very wet June and everyone was sick of it, including Isabelle. The wipers droned on and on, reception for the radio was awful, the tape player was broken and CD players hadn't been invented the year her car rolled off the assembly line. With rain obliterating the scenery, there was precious little to occupy her thoughts.

Except for lost love.

Marnie, standing in the passenger seat with her front feet up on the armrest, threw Isabelle an over-the-shoulder glance as though she sensed in which direction Isabelle's thoughts had been drifting.

"I know you always loved him, maybe even more than you love me," Isabelle said. She often talked to her dog. When Marnie actually bothered to listen, it seemed as if she understood just about everything.

But that was crazy.

For the first time in years, Isabelle thought about her twenty-second birthday and the special gift Rick had chosen for her.

A dog.

A tiny, yappy little dog with enough personality for a whole litter. He'd chosen her himself, named her after a character in his favorite Hitchcock movie, kept her for two weeks until Isabelle's late September birthday rolled around and then handed her over with a red bow tied around her neck.

Marnie.

Man and dog had bonded in that two-week period and Isabelle always suspected the dog would have preferred staying with Rick. He'd been living on the coast at the time and spent the summers working for his dad, living in the ramshackle apartment above the boatyard his father owned. Lots of activity and noise, Rick in sight every moment of the day and night, the ocean a sand dune away — Marnie had loved it.

"No need to feel embarrassed," Isabelle added. "I don't really blame you."

Marnie pressed her long nose against the window, effectively turning her back.

Thinking of her perpetually out-of-sorts landlady, Isabelle added, "I'd just like you to remember who defends you against Mrs.

Pughill."

Marnie seemed to be engaged in some deep doggy thought and obviously didn't want to consider Mrs. Pughill.

Isabelle sighed. Face it. Seeing Rick had rattled her. She'd forgotten how she used to feel when he looked at her, how she used to wait anxiously just to hear his voice on the telephone, how the feel of his skin against hers used to make every female cell in her body shout for joy.

She'd forgotten how desperately she had once loved him. She'd also forgotten how completely he'd broken her heart.

Marnie licked her elbow and brought her back to the present.

"I hate to remind you of this, but he left you, too," Isabelle mumbled.

Marnie stretched her throat and howled.

When Rick Manning exited the elevator on the seventh floor, he found his mind still filled with images of Isabelle. If anything, she looked younger than she had four years before. Lustrous, dark brown hair, eyes like melted chocolate, creamy skin — Isabelle was a looker.

And she didn't know it. She never had. Judging from what he saw today, she still dressed like an adolescent, she still didn't worry about makeup and hairdos. Her beauty was obviously more luck than design.

He was surprised by how much he'd missed her the past few years.

Well, why not? At one time, she'd been everything to him. The morning and the night, the sun and the stars, everything. He'd thought they'd last forever.

So what had gone wrong?

He'd decided to go to law school, that's what.

He'd decided he didn't want to live on the coast and design boats. Any other woman in the world would have been relieved that her beloved wanted a secure future. Not Isabelle. He wanted some of the finer things in life and that took a decent income with a future. He also wanted to make a difference in peoples' lives, something he had to admit he found damn difficult to articulate. The more he argued his side of things, the more she withdrew, claiming his dreams sounded soulless to her and she just couldn't talk about it.

He knew she thought he was the one who had left. But the truth was less clear than that — they'd just sort of both left each other.

And she'd taken "his" dog.

Her dog, yes, but his dog, too.

Some loves weren't meant to be. He'd admitted that to himself long ago, and seeing Isabelle today only confirmed it. They were oil and water, a lamb and a tiger, though when she wasn't on the defensive, she was the most irresistible, warmhearted woman in the world.

He hadn't know she'd moved to Seaport. That probably meant she saw his father once in a while. The two of them had always been close, something he'd thought was great — at first. Later, it had seemed as if they'd ganged up on him. He felt a twinge somewhere in his chest.

At least he now knew Isabelle no longer cared about him one way or another, and that was something of a relief.

Life goes on, his twice-divorced and once-widowed father used to say so often it had taken Rick years to realize the old man hadn't come up with the cliché on his own.

The old man was right.

Life goes on . . .

With that in mind, Rick knocked on the door of 702 and waited.

Chapter Two

Before Isabelle drove home, she stopped by the grocery store. The long drive to and from Portland plus the hours spent consoling Heather had left her feeling as washed out as the pale sky. And ravenous. Normally, Heather made delicious little snacks for them to munch during their visits. Things with mushrooms, things with shrimp, things with cheese. Okay, Isabelle didn't have the slightest idea what any of them were, she just knew she loved each and every bite-size morsel!

But Heather had been too upset that day to cook. Hence procuring dinner for both herself and Marnie was taking on a whole new importance.

She shopped carefully, as money was always tight. Thankfully, her needs were simple.

The curtain in the front window of her landlady's side of their shared duplex slid open as Isabelle pulled into the driveway. With a resigned sigh, she waved as she got out of the car. Marnie bounded to freedom, making straight for the flower bed, which left Isabelle caught between a rock and a hard place. Did she call to her wayward dog and bring attention to the fact that Marnie was now watering Mrs. Pughill's prize roses, or did she pretend she didn't notice and hope the older woman didn't, either?

Since when was there anything that went on around the duplex that Bertha Pughill or her ancient toy poodle, Ignatz, didn't notice?

She called Marnie.

Marnie, for once, came immediately, and together they brought inside two of the bags from the grocery store. Isabelle heard Marnie exit through the doggy flap inserted in the kitchen door. As it emptied into a fenced, and semiprivate, backyard, she put the dog out of her mind.

After stowing the groceries, Isabelle filled Marnie's bowl and set it on the floor. It took her a few seconds to realize that Marnie hadn't come shooting inside the flap the moment she heard the kibble hit the bowl. Most unusual. Isabelle opened the back door. No Marnie.

She walked the perimeter of the wire

fence. No doubt Marnie could jump it or dig under it, but so far the dog had been satisfied to stay within the fence. At times, it seemed to Isabelle that her terrier understood how impossible life would be for both of them if she took to escaping the yard on her own.

So, where was she now?

Isabelle quickly traversed the house to the front door and tore it open. And there was Marnie, sitting on the doormat, a newspaper spread open by her feet.

It looked as if Marnie was smiling!

"Oh, no!" Isabelle cried, automatically glancing next door to see if Mrs. Pughill was watching. She could hear the faint sounds of Ignatz barking, but so far, so good; no Mrs. Pughill. Isabelle picked up the paper and brought it inside, noting as she did that it was the Portland paper.

"First you shred it at Heather's, and now you're out stealing the darn thing!" she told Marnie who, as usual, didn't look the least bit repentant. "What in the world has gotten into you today?"

Marnie barked once. Decisively.

"Maybe I'll just read the headlines before I take it back to Mrs. Pughill," Isabelle said, glancing down. At that exact moment, a rapacious series of knocks announced the gig was up. Marnie barked furiously. Isabelle tried to shush her.

"I know you're in there!" Mrs. Pughill cried. "Open up or I'll use my key! Miss Winters! Open up."

"Can't it wait?" Isabelle called, looking for somewhere to ditch the paper which seemed to be opening and spreading, separating into sections, becoming more and more cumbersome as though possessed with a life force of its own.

"It most certainly cannot. You're harboring a thief, young lady. Now open up!"

Isabelle glared at Marnie, who looked more discouraged than contrite.

"Oh, what the hell," she said as she opened the front door.

Mrs. Pughill pretty much fit her name: the face of a pug and a body as round and lumpy as a hill. Put her in a battered black robe with moth-eaten socks on her feet, add a cap of impossibly brassy hair and small eyes currently glittering with fury, and the woman was a tour de force.

Behind the glowering landlady lurked an ancient poodle that defied the adage that pets and owners grow to look alike. Ignatz probably didn't weigh five pounds soaking wet. His eyes always looked watery and a tuft of smoky gray fur erupted from the top of his head like a plume of frizzy feathers.

Both Mrs. Pughill and Ignatz bared yellow teeth.

"I might never have known what happened to my newspaper tonight if Ignatz hadn't warned me there was a thief about!" Mrs. Pughill sputtered indignantly. "The little dear is an excellent watchdog."

The "little dear" issued a sharp bark.

There was no use denying it, Isabelle thought, seeing as she was holding the evidence. She offered it to her landlady.

Marnie growled.

Mrs. Pughill threw up both hands as though Isabelle was trying to pawn off an oozing fish head. "Gracious, no," she said. "You keep it. Look at it! I don't want it after your mutt slobbered all over it."

"I'll wrap it in a paper towel," Isabelle said with forbearance.

"I'd still have to touch it to read it," Mrs. Pughill said. "I always read my horoscopes so I can plot my day. Madame Hortense is a genius. Now what will I do?"

Isabelle had half a mind to tell her what she could do, but instead she rolled the paper and plucked a couple of tissues from a nearby box. Wrapping them around the paper, she forced it into Mrs. Pughill's hands.

"I can't read this," the landlady insisted. "I distinctly told you when you moved in that your dog had to be well mannered like my Ignatz."

"I know you did," Isabelle managed to squeak out. "I'm very sorry."

"Sorry doesn't help me read the horoscopes," Mrs. Pughill, who was turning out to be as tenacious as a pug, insisted.

"Then I'll give you the money to buy yourself a brand-new paper," Isabelle said. "You can have two newspapers and twice as many horoscopes!"

Marnie growled again, this time with meaning.

Mrs. Pughill cast the terrier an alarmed look as Ignatz scooted behind her legs. She said, "The paper cost one dollar and fifty cents at the store on the corner."

"I'll go get the newspaper and deliver it to you."

"The money will be good enough," Mrs. Pughill said. "I'll buy my own paper."

Sure you will, Isabelle grumbled internally, but managed to say, "I'll bring the money right over." As Marnie had started growling again, Isabelle quickly closed her door.

"What's with you today?" she snapped.

Marnie cocked her head to one side.

"Oh, never mind."

Once she found the proper change, Isabelle locked Marnie inside and went next door. She left a few minutes later, ears still ringing about the consequences of any further bad behavior by her dog.

Maybe she should try to find a new place to live this summer, she thought fleetingly, and let it go. Summer vacationers would snap up all the rentals. She'd have to wait until it was almost fall. The thought of getting a classroom ready and moving into a new apartment at the same time had all the appeal of covering herself with honey and standing next to a bear. Besides, hadn't she had to look at every vacancy in town to find this place? Affordable apartments that allowed pets were few and far between.

Back home, she found Marnie staring up at the small antique desk Rick had given Isabelle for Christmas way back when. That meant she was either interested in the computer or the telephone. As the answering machine light was blinking, Isabelle figured out which it must be. "I'll check that out later," she said. "Right now I'm hungry enough to gnaw on my own arm."

As she walked into the kitchen, she continued her one-sided conversation with Marnie. "We're just lucky Mrs. Pughill is lazy," she said as she took a frozen entree out of the freezer and popped it in the microwave. "She won't kick me out of here until she has to."

She glanced down at the dog food bowl, expecting to see Marnie's back, instead finding a bowl still brimming with kibble. Curious, Isabelle walked back to the living room. Marnie was right where Isabelle had left her, staring at the blinking light on the answering machine.

"You are not the only stubborn one in this family," Isabelle said, turning right around and attending to the beeping of the microwave. She took out her steaming serving of pasta and shrimp and sat down at the table. The food tasted good and hot. Isabelle liked microwavable food, the more ready to eat right out of its own container, the better. It was one of the indulgences she allowed herself, and one of the perks of living alone.

And that made her think of Rick; the man was no slouch in the kitchen. He'd stirred them up some truly delicious dishes. Two years they'd gone out, two years of discovering all there was to know about him, two years of shared meals and experiences, of weaving dreams of the future, of wild romance.

Since they'd parted after college, Isabelle

had dated, but so far hadn't connected with anyone the way she'd connected with Rick. Still, she was young, there was time, what was the rush? For now, getting through the rest of the school year and reconnecting with friends she was too busy to see during the school year would keep her busy. And who knew what kind of support Heather would need as the weeks rolled by?

If she had spare time, maybe she'd date some.

Maybe not.

Usually, she didn't think about romance much. This uncharacteristic melancholy she was experiencing was no doubt the result of seeing Rick again.

God, was he gorgeous!

A voice suddenly boomed from the other room. Startled, Isabelle dropped her fork. If Mrs. Pughill had unlocked her front door and entered without knocking, Isabelle was ready to call the police. She marched into the living room under a head of steam.

Marnie stood on the desk, wedged in between the phone and the computer, her lilac-colored, heart-shaped identification tag catching the overhead light. The dog was staring at the answering machine from which came Heather's anguished voice. Somehow, the little dog had figured out how to push the Play button!

". . . the paper, today's paper," Heather was saying. "Now we've both lost the only man we ever loved. . . ."

The message clicked off on a sob.

Marnie jumped to the floor as Isabelle sank down on a nearby chair, her stomach suddenly roiling. Heather had to be talking about Rick. He was the only man she'd ever loved, and Heather knew it. Had something happened to him? And then she remembered she'd seen him that very afternoon *after* the paper was delivered.

She pushed the Play button again.

"Isabelle? Aren't you home yet? Never mind, I just read about Rick. He's engaged. He's getting married this winter! Did you know? I read it in the paper, today's paper. Now we've both lost the only man we ever loved. . . ."

Isabelle stared at her little dog.

"How did you know?" she whispered.

Marnie wagged her four-inch tail and managed to look smug.

I'd like to set the record straight about a few things.

First. I don't love Rick better than Isabelle. Where did she ever get such a crazy idea?

Second. I think I may be psychic.

Third. Note to Ignatz: nobody likes a pushy poodle.

About the psychic thing — how else would you explain the fact that Rick's picture showed up in the newspaper when I'd been dreaming about him? How else to explain the way he appeared in Heather's lobby once I started concentrating on his photograph? And how about Heather's phone call? Explain that!

Okay, okay, enough.

I have to admit that Heather's news hit me hard. I hadn't seen that coming.

Isabelle, after hearing Heather's message, ran out of the apartment and returned a few minutes later with the newspaper. At last! I felt like cheering. I could have told her to start her search on page one, but frankly, she hadn't been paying very good attention that day so I left her to her own devices. Eventually she found the right section. It took her a moment to read whatever was there, then she folded the newspaper down on itself and sat like a block of granite for twenty minutes.

I was seriously considering tearing apart a pillow to snap her out of it when she threw the paper to the floor and stomped off to her bed, where she buried herself under her covers.

At that point, I looked at the newspaper.

The same picture of Rick from the front page was also buried inside, but it was bigger. Next to his photo was one of a brunette with a glancing resemblance to Isabelle. It didn't take a rocket scientist to figure out who the little lady was.

How could he!

Why would he?

How did I stop this?

Good gad, had the man gone bonkers?

He was supposed to rediscover the fact that he loves Isabelle. And me, of course. He was supposed to come to his senses. When he saw her — and me — he was supposed to realize that he'd wasted the last four years, that it was time to stop fooling around! He was not supposed to get himself engaged to some pale imitation of the real thing. He was not supposed to be on the verge of leaving us forever.

And that's when I remembered what he'd whispered close to my ear at Heather's building.

"Take good care of her," he'd said.

Does a man say something like that about a woman he isn't crazy about? Grant you, human beings sometimes befuddle me, but that comment reeked of sentimentality, did it not?

I couldn't think straight!

Of course! I hadn't eaten dinner. I needed sustenance. It took me a while to plow through the bowl of kibble Isabelle had set out for me.

Midway through a nice after-dinner drink of water (Isabelle always leaves me a bowl, but I prefer the dripping kitchen faucet), I thought I detected a noise. Cocking an ear, I listened intently until I recognized the sound.

Muffled sobs. Isabelle was crying.

I jumped off the kitchen counter and trotted into the bedroom, staring up at the lump on the bed.

What could I do beyond offering moral support? That's all well and good, but I felt the need for action. I wanted to morph into Superdog, I wanted to make this thing right.

After a few more moments, I jumped up on the bed and cuddled close against Isabelle's swathed legs. Normally, she would have scolded me and told me to get off the bed.

But that night, she freed a hand from the tangle of sheets and blankets, and rested it on top of my head. Her fingers stroked my fur as I rested my chin on her hip. Gradually, her sobbing faded away and her breathing slowed down.

It's times like these that make a dog proud to be . . . well, a dog.

Maybe I wasn't Superdog, but I was psychic. Probably. The jury was still out on that one, though the evidence did seem to support my supposition. Hey, I hadn't lived for two weeks of my impressionable youth with a guy dreaming about being a lawyer without some of it rubbing off!

All I had to do was will something to happen. Anything would be better than nothing. Feeling that I was close to figuring this thing out, I went ahead and caught a little shut-eye. It had been a very long day.

Rick woke up the next morning and laid very still, the impressions of a dream still fresh in his mind. He was at his dad's boathouse, a place he hadn't set foot in since the day he and Isabelle had parted company. Isabelle was standing in the door, backlit by sunlight, her expression impossible to read. His father was standing beside a half-finished boat and he was smiling. Smiling! And Marnie was there, bigger than real life, damn near the size of a pony!

No matter how hard he concentrated, he couldn't remember any further details. What remained was an antsy feeling in the pit of his stomach.

As he showered, he kept thinking about his dad. The old man built sailboats. They weren't huge boats, but they were renowned for their beauty and seaworthiness. They also came with a sky-high price tag but made his father precious little profit. For his dad, it was a labor of love. Why couldn't his father understand that Rick wanted to be one of the guys buying the boat, not building it? And why couldn't he understand that perhaps Rick's labor of love might take a whole different form?

With a longing ache, he recalled the many times Isabelle had pitched in to help on one of his dad's boats. She and his dad had cracked a million bad jokes as Rick played the part of straight man.

He also recalled the long walks he and Isabelle would take in the evening. Marnie had been little more than a puppy at the time, a blur of white-and-tan fur, trotting along beside them, little front legs straight, little flap ears bouncing.

Isabelle always seemed to be bundled up to within an inch of her life because that north wind blew cold even in August. She would cling to his arm, bury her chilly nose against his neck and meet his kisses with lips as warm as spring rain.

For three glorious summers, they'd lived in Seaport, him over his father's boatyard where he worked to earn enough money for the coming semester, her at a summer school for special needs kids. She'd had a scholarship, so she hadn't had to work for money and could volunteer her time.

They'd worked hard every day at their

respective jobs, and then spent every evening together, at his place, her place or on the beach. It had been a time out of time, he could see now.

As he knotted his tie, he glanced at the picture of Chloe on his dresser. She was the senior partner's daughter, a recent graduate who sashayed around the office dressed like a million bucks, every hair in place. She'd set her sights on him the moment she saw him. Coming on the heels of Isabelle's disdain, Chloe's infatuation had been good for his ego.

Now Chloe wanted to get married.

Should a man engaged to be married be having dreams about an old love?

He thought he knew why Isabelle was suddenly on his mind. She was unfinished business. Running into her the day before in the lobby of Chloe's building had been accidental, but perhaps providential, as well. He would have told her about his engagement then, but she'd gotten kind of weird when she talked about her being a teacher and him being a lawyer.

Why did she have a chip on her shoulder? How could she misread his interest as some kind of insult?

Never mind, that wasn't the issue. Since Isabelle lived out of town, he thought it doubtful she'd see the announcement in the paper. He didn't like her finding out he was getting married during some gossipy call from a friend.

Would she give a hoot one way or another?

Doubtful, but he felt funny about it and that was enough. He would tell her himself. She could be as snippy as she wanted, he would take it like a man, it would be over.

Glancing at his appointment book, he saw that he had a court date early in the afternoon, but that after that he was free. He would drive to the coast and kill two birds with one stone. He'd find Isabelle and tell her his good news, then he'd drive by his dad's boatyard. This thing between them had gone on long enough.

As he poured a bowl of cereal and dug in the fridge for the milk, Rick felt a sense of anticipation rise in his chest.

That was understandable; it had been a long time since he'd been to the beach.

Chapter Three

"Your dog has been barking all day!" Mrs. Pughill announced the moment Isabelle got out of her car.

It had been a long day, filled with misadventure. Her usually well-behaved class had been impossible, hyped up on the sugar doughnuts an enthusiastic parent had delivered midmorning. A little girl had brought her pet rat, which escaped during recess and took an hour to find, and still another child had brought a trumpet to show and tell.

The little boy did not seem to be musically inclined. Half the school had thought there was a fire drill going on. Add a midday call from a frantic Heather who begged Isabelle to come back to Portland for additional hand-holding, an irritable principal about two weeks away from giving birth to twins, and presto: chaos.

"I don't hear anything, Mrs. Pughill," Isabelle said firmly, ignoring the muffled "Arf,

arf, arf," coming from behind her front door.

"My horoscope said a loved one would be taken ill and your mutt is driving my poor Ignatz crazy," Mrs. Pughill insisted. Ignatz, hiding behind his master's swollen ankles, growled for emphasis. "What's wrong with *your* dog?"

"That's a very good question," Isabelle mused, though she thought she knew the answer. Afraid to let the dog wander freely in the backyard — Marnie having proven the night before she could jump the fence at will — Isabelle had locked her inside. Undoubtedly, the poor little thing needed a patch of grass and some privacy. "I'll take care of it," she promised, letting herself into her half of the duplex and closing the door firmly behind her.

She expected to find Marnie with metaphorically crossed knees, waiting anxiously by the latched dog flap. She did not expect to find her sitting on the desk.

Marnie yapped.

"Your current behavior is unacceptable," Isabelle said as she dropped her purse and a stack of books on the small table by the door. "You have to stop tormenting Mrs. Pughill. You're going to get us evicted if you keep this up. I think I need to find you a good dog shrink."

The light on the answering machine was blinking again. As Isabelle reached to push the Play button, she noticed her hairbrush sitting on the desk along with a tube of lipstick.

"How did these things get here?" Isabelle mumbled, as she pushed the button.

It was Rick's voice that called out this time. "Isabelle? I need to see you. Expect me about four."

That was all. Just like him to issue an order and expect her to fall into line. She should get in the car and leave. She couldn't imagine why he thought he needed to see her and wasn't the least bit anxious to find out.

Well, maybe a little.

Glancing at her watch, she saw that it was five minutes after four. The thought of leaving before he got there skittered across her mind again, this time sounding even better.

As if commenting on her thoughts, Marnie yipped, then using her nose, nudged the hairbrush Isabelle's direction. It ran into the tube of lipstick, causing the lipstick to roll off the desk. Isabelle caught the gold cylinder before it hit the floor.

She stared at the lipstick. She stared at the hairbrush. She stared at the dog. Honestly, it appeared as if the little animal had understood Rick's message and had retrieved these personal grooming items for Isabelle to use in order to spruce herself up before he arrived!

"I'm the one who needs the shrink," Isabelle said as the doorbell rang.

"And that's got to be Rick," she added, staring at the front door. Mrs. Pughill never rang the bell, preferring instead to bang on the door like the vice squad. Isabelle set aside the lipstick as Marnie jumped to the floor. By the time Isabelle got to the door, the little dog was standing on her hind feet, front paws against the wood as though straining to see out the peephole.

With a sigh, Isabelle opened the door.

Marnie bounced at Rick who caught her in his arms.

"Hi," he said over Marnie's back.

Isabelle stared at him, tempted to be curt, tempted to tell him to put her dog down and go away. She dreaded the impending conversation though she couldn't imagine what it might concern.

"You don't live far from my father's place," he added.

"Just a couple of blocks," Isabelle said.

"I had no idea."

"That's because you haven't been to see

him for umpteen years."

"You know that's not entirely fair. I've tried. He's still mad at me for . . ." His voice trailed off as he apparently decided not to mention the reason his father was still mad. He knew, Isabelle knew, everyone knew. Rick said, "That's part of the reason I'm here, Isabelle. May I come inside and talk to you?"

They both looked over at the sound of Mrs. Pughill exiting her side of the duplex. "I hope you're here to take that annoying little scoundrel away," Mrs. Pughill said, fists planted on her ample hips. "That dog barked all afternoon. Ignatz is still reeling. Madame Hortense foretold it."

Ignatz, lurking in the open doorway, bared yellow teeth and growled.

Marnie yipped once. Rick hushed her but turned questioning eyes to Isabelle. She shrugged. She did not want to talk in front of Mrs. Pughill. She also didn't want Rick inside her home. Snatching Marnie's leash from its hook by the door, she said, "Let's go for a walk."

As Isabelle had pointed out, it had been a long time since Rick had been in Seaport, and as he walked, he took deep breaths of salty, tangy air, so redolent of the ocean that it had a taste of its own.

Off in the distance, he could hear the sound of the bell buoy marking the entrance to the short jetty that protected the harbor. The clanking noise grew louder as they walked toward the beach. The cawing of gulls and the distant rumble of high tide against the rocky shore to the north added more notes to the endless symphony of the small seaside town.

It felt odd to be here walking beside Isabelle again. In the past, he would have had an arm around her shoulders or her arm would have been looped through his. As it was, his hands were shoved deep in his jean pockets and an important foot or so of space separated their bodies. If one of them accidentally moved too close, the other shied away. The gap between them might be unacknowledged, but it was inviolate.

They passed a weathered gray house, flowerpots brimming with bright yellow and orange nasturtiums, Shasta daisies bobbing in the fresh breeze, the foliage of lavender plants silvery green against an old fence that had once sported a coat of white paint. His dad's place was a block over, he realized with a start. As a kid, he'd ridden his bike by this old house a million times.

"You look nostalgic," Isabelle said.

"Mrs. Polk lives in this house," he said, pausing to stare up at the faded blue door.

"Not anymore. She died last year. Her sons are fighting about what to do with the house. It's empty right now."

"It's a neat old place," he said.

"That's the trouble," Isabelle said. "The house is old and in need of repair. It's not worth a fraction of what the land on which it sits is worth. One son wants to keep the house as is and rent it out to summer vacationers, the other wants to bulldoze it off the face of the earth, build a rack of look-alike condos."

He stared down at her. It wasn't hard to figure out where she stood on the issue. Isabelle didn't like change, she didn't approve of progress.

She smiled at him as though she knew what he was thinking. Wearing a soft, blue cotton blouse with a fluttery scarf tied around her throat, she looked totally at home in Seaport. The shirt, belted into khaki slacks, showcased her trim figure. Windblown tendrils of brown hair teased her cheeks, and she absently brushed them away. He noticed that maturity was beginning to hone the rounded contours of her pretty face, and the aura of impatience that had so suffused her the day before seemed to have abated.

She appeared happy, he thought. Was it because she'd found work she adored? *Or was it because he had come to see her? Was there a chance she still cared about him?*

But that would be awful. He needed to tell her about Chloe and his engagement, he needed to squelch any hope she might have that he was there because he wanted them to get back together. He cleared his throat and blurted it out. "I'm getting married in December."

Marnie's "Woof!" sounded like a foghorn.

Isabelle said, "I know. I read about it in yesterday's newspaper. Your intended's family is quite prominent. It was a big write-up."

"Yeah," he said, suddenly feeling foolish. She hadn't been having romantic thoughts about him, after all. Maybe there was someone new in her life, maybe that's why her skin and eyes glowed.

She started walking again and he caught up. She said, "So, you're marrying the senior partner's daughter, is that right?"

He mumbled, "That's right."

"Congratulations," she said, and then stopped walking and turned to face him. "Rick? Is that why you wanted to see me? To tell me about your engagement?" Laughing, she added, "It is, isn't it, I can tell by the expression on your face! Oh, that's funny. Sweet, I guess, in a kind of egotistical way, but funny. Did you think I'd fall apart or something?"

Marnie, standing between them, started whining.

For something to do, he leaned over and patted the dog's wiry head. When he straightened up, Rick said, "Of course not. I wanted your help in deciding how to approach my dad, that's all. You and he were always close. I figure you still see him occasionally."

"Every weekend. He has the same caffeine habit I do. We meet at the Coffee Hut, that old place down near the beach."

"Dad's never forgiven me for not becoming a yacht designer," Rick said, a trifle alarmed at the thought of Isabelle and his father drinking coffee together, chatting, discussing him, maybe. He added, "The old man hates lawyers. A couple of divorces will do that to a man. He's never forgiven me for not staying here and —"

"Marrying me, go ahead and say it," Isabelle said. She laughed again. "Your dad is opinionated but he loves you."

"I hope so," Rick said, not at all sure.

Isabelle bit her lip, and then looked at him

through her lashes. It was a look he recalled with a sudden burst of fondness, her unsure look, as unconscious as it was beguiling. "What is it?" he asked.

"Nothing really."

"Just tell me," he insisted.

"It's nothing. Okay, it's something, but not much of anything."

"Isabelle —"

"Okay. It's just that . . . well, building boats is hard work. Go easy on him. He seems kind of . . . delicate to me."

"Delicate? Are you kidding? My father?"

"He's had high blood pressure for years. He takes medication — when he remembers. He won't go to the doctor for a checkup. He promises me that he isn't smoking anymore, but I smell it on his clothes. I worry about him, that's all. I'm really glad you're going to go see him."

"I am, too," he said, alarmed at what she'd told him. It was just like the old man to ignore his health. He thought he was invincible. Grabbing Isabelle's hand, he said, "I'm going to go see him right now and you're coming with me."

"No, Rick. This doesn't concern me. This is between you and him. I'd only get in the way."

"Ha!" he said. "You'll be the only reason

he'll let me in the door."

"No. You need to apologize in private —"

"Apologize? Who said anything about apologizing? What have I done that I need to apologize for? Lived my own life? Made my own decisions?"

"Now —"

"He's the one who should apologize."

She narrowed her eyes. "If you feel this way, why are you even bothering? You go in there with that attitude, and he'll kick you out. How many years will you let pass the next time? How many years do you think he has left?"

Rick swore under his breath. "Do you see why I need you to be there, Isabelle? Swallowing my pride is hard."

"Maybe there's a little more of your dad in you than you're comfortable with," she said.

"Don't be nasty. Just come with me."

"No. Just be patient with him. You'll be fine —"

Marnie, who had been sitting quietly as though listening to their every word, chose that moment to lunge. Maybe she'd seen a cat or another dog. All Rick knew was that Isabelle was apparently unprepared. The leash flew out of her hand as the dog bounded down the sidewalk, looking back over her shoulder toward them, barking, heedless of the busy intersection less than a block away. A cacophony of backyard barking resounded up and down the street as it seemed every dog within hearing distance somehow knew the moment Marnie gained her freedom.

"Marnie!" Isabelle shouted.

Rick was already running. He could hear Isabelle's footsteps pounding the sidewalk behind him.

Oh, to run!

Just run. Full tilt, flat out run.

Cheered on by a chorus of your peers, the wind in your face, your paws flying; what could be better?

Having people chase you just adds to the thrill. A leash flapping behind you just makes the whole thing more exciting.

I heard Isabelle shout, and felt a momentary pang at disobeying her, but honestly, the joy of running just got the better of me. Oh, so did my determination to get my recalcitrant mistress to go along with Rick. I wanted her by his side, I wanted her to recall how much fun they had together. That couldn't happen if the two of them went their separate ways.

I'd quit running eventually, but not until I'd led them to Rick's dad's boatyard. Once there,

Isabelle would hang around. If not, I'd think of something else.

Now, where was that place?

That's when I turned to check out the street ahead and found my course was about to take me smack dab into the path of a great big truck. . . .

Isabelle saw Marnie spring into the street at the same time she became aware of a big delivery truck lumbering down Main. It was too late for her to do a thing to save her dog!

She screamed "Marnie!" or maybe she screamed, "Rick!" At the same time she heard the blare of a horn and the squeal of brakes, she saw Rick fly off the sidewalk, arms stretched out in front of him, in what she assumed to be a last-ditch effort to grab Marnie's leash. She heard a horrible thud. Heart in throat, she covered the distance to the street with feet that seemed to have been suddenly dipped in lead.

By the time she got there, the truck driver was out of his cab, his face as pale as sea foam. Marnie was standing beside Rick, barking at the traffic, the driver, the world in general. Rick was sitting alarmingly close to the front wheels of the truck, knees bent, head down. Bloody scrapes ran up his arms.

There was gravel embedded in one minced palm while the other hand gripped Marnie's leash so tightly his knuckles showed white.

"Are you okay?" she cried, stepping out onto the lane nearest the sidewalk. Another blast of a horn stopped her in her tracks. A new set of brakes squealed in protest. "Watch out!" the truck driver hollered as he pulled her to the relative safety of the inside lane. His idling truck made an imposing roadblock as an irate driver gunned his engine and whizzed past.

"Thanks," Isabelle whispered, trembling now.

"What's wrong with you people?" the trucker shrieked. "Do you have some kind of suicide pact? I almost wiped out your friend here and, lady, you came this close to being a hood ornament!"

It wasn't hard for Isabelle to look apologetic, embarrassed, grateful and relieved all at once. Kneeling in front of Rick, she dredged up a smile. "Are you okay?" she asked again.

A scrape ran along his left cheek. Blood dripped from his chin. He said, "I'm just dandy. You?"

Marnie wiggled in close and licked his hand. Isabelle's irritation with her clueless pet turned into a wave of tenderness. The little dog led a sheltered life, always locked in a yard or in the house unless secured to the end of a leash. Unless she was on a beach, that is, but there weren't any cars on the beach. She didn't know about cars. It had been a close call.

Patting her pet's wiry head, she looked at Rick. He looked dazed.

"I don't know what's gotten into Marnie lately," Isabelle said. "She seems to be . . . out of control."

Isabelle and Rick both stared at Marnie, who stared back at them with guileless black eyes.

Taking Rick's arm, Isabelle helped him stand, stumbling a little as he momentarily rested his weight on her shoulder. When he handed her Marnie's leash, she could see his other hand also sported abrasions, though not as severe.

"Your reflexes saved us," Rick told the truck driver. "Thanks."

"Thank my mechanic," the trucker said as he climbed back in his cab. "He's the one who takes care of my brakes!" Waiting for a clearing in the rush hour traffic, Rick limped to the sidewalk, with Isabelle at his side and Marnie prancing out in front. The truck roared away with a blast of its horn.

"Your slacks are ruined," Isabelle said once they were safe.

As Rick looked down at the shredded knees, Isabelle unwound the silk scarf she wore around her neck. She dabbed at his chin, which had stopped bleeding on its own, then wound the scarf around Rick's hand. His gaze met hers, and for a moment or two, time did an odd kind of spinning thing; there was no present or past, certainly no future. She held his hand in hers, their eyes locked. In a perverse way, she felt closer to him than she ever had.

Marnie had the gall to bark impatiently! Their hands parted, the moment was gone, Isabelle was left facing a near stranger engaged to be married to another woman.

Looking down at Marnie, Isabelle grumbled, "Hush." She turned back to Rick and added, "I have antiseptic and bandages back at my place —"

He suddenly wasn't paying the slightest bit of attention to her. She followed his gaze, curious as to what had him so mesmerized.

She hadn't realized that the cross street was right across the busy road from Rick's father's boatyard. Rick's father was standing in a small crowd of onlookers gathered on the opposite side of the four-lane highway. Apparently the screech of brakes and the honking horns had brought him outside to see what was going on.

"Maybe my tattered condition will soften the old geezer's heart," Rick said softly. "This whole incident might turn out to be a blessing in disguise. Let's go."

Marnie, apparently taking credit for the "blessing in disguise," turned a complete circle, thereby tangling herself in the leash.

Isabelle used the time it took her to extricate Marnie's legs and feet from the coils of cord to consider her options.

She could go home where she belonged.

Yet, despite the near-death experiences, wasn't she — in some perverse way — enjoying herself?

And what about Rick's dad? Wouldn't her presence serve as a buffer between father and son? Besides, he'd seen her now, how rude would it be to suddenly disappear without even saying, "Hello"?

Pretty darn rude.

The only thing of which she was certain was that she would not stick around to hear Rick describe his fiancée to his father. At that point, she would beat a hasty retreat.

"Let's go," she said, immediately feeling as if her words were loaded with meaning.

Chapter Four

Despite meeting Carl Manning at the Coffee Hut on a regular basis, it had been years since Isabelle had been inside his boatworks. She drove past it going to and from the school where she worked, but all that was visible from the road were a half-dozen rotting old boats tucked up against the fence, all of which seemed to be permanently drydocked.

Inside the gate, a marine railway brought both fishing boats and pleasure craft from Seaport's small harbor up to dry land where the yard crew and owners could repair cracked planks, work on engines and rigging and reapply bottom paint. Off to the side was a huge old wooden structure, outfitted as a workshop below with living quarters built into the loft above.

Situated on the ground floor of the building there was always a wooden sailboat in some stage of construction. Carl built them on commission, taking a year or more to finish one, putting his heart and soul into every detail. Most were under thirty feet, all were works of art. It amazed Isabelle that someone as surly as Carl could 1) have been married three times and 2) build such lovely yachts.

Carl Manning had bought the place the year after his third wife, Rick's mother, had died. Rick had been eight years old at the time, so for all intents and purposes, he'd grown up at the boatyard. It had been assumed he'd take over some day and toward this goal, had worked long hours for his dad. When he'd insisted on going to college, his father had called it a waste of money, softening only when Rick decided to study yacht design. When Rick had changed his mind and gone off to law school, Carl Manning had thrown a doozy of a snit.

He met them now on the sidewalk, out in front of the row of decaying boats. Smiling at Isabelle, he glared at his son and finally said, "What the hell happened to you?"

"It's nice to see you, too," Rick said, his voice taut.

"What are you doing here?"

"What do you think I'm doing here?"

"Looks to me like you're trying to get

yourself run over."

Isabelle, hoping to defuse the situation said, "My dog got away from me. If it weren't for Rick's quick thinking, Marnie could have been killed." She took Rick's arm a little too enthusiastically. She'd forgotten he was wounded and she felt him flinch.

"Hmmph!" Carl said.

"I could use some bandages to patch him up," Isabelle persisted.

"Hmmph!" Carl repeated. He turned abruptly and led the way into the yard, past the boats up on their cradles, into the building. It was dark by comparison to the bright day outside.

The older man was nearing seventy. He'd put on some weight recently while his wild thatch of white hair was as unruly as ever. He wore what he always wore, black denim pants and a shirt made from blue-and-white ticking, held together with red suspenders. Add a navy pea jacket in the winter and worn leather boots any time of the year, and that was his uniform. Isabelle couldn't recall seeing him dressed any other way.

Along with an extensive workshop, Carl's newest boat occupied much of the floor space. The hull, supported by a superstructure of scaffolding, had ladders rising to the decks fore and aft. Though still unrigged, the yacht looked as though it was nearing completion. Coils of rigging, stacks of lumber and dozens upon dozens of old boxes full of ship-related treasures were stacked against a far wall. Nearby, a long laminated spar rested atop several sawhorses.

Rick reached toward the glistening wood.

"Don't touch that!" his dad snapped. "What's wrong with you, boy? Been away from boats so long you can't even tell when the varnish is still wet?"

"Yeah," Rick growled as he lowered his hand. "I spent my whole childhood around boats, but after a few years away from here, I can't tell when the varnish is wet. Sure, Dad."

Isabelle winced. When Rick glanced her way, she did her best to look encouraging. She saw the knot in his jaw relax and in a more moderate voice, he added, "This boat is a real beauty. Looks like the one you built five years ago for that lawyer up in Seattle."

"He died last spring. Heart attack."

Rick said, "Oh. Well, I'm sorry —"

"Life goes on," his father said. "This boat is for a dentist down in Eureka, California. I've got the stuff you need to patch up those scrapes," he added before taking the rickety stairs up to his apartment two at a time.

The look Rick gave Isabelle spoke volumes. It said, *I thought you told me my old man was delicate!*

She shrugged.

Frowning, he followed his dad.

Oh, the temptation to tiptoe away and leave these two grumps to their own devices! When Marnie paused on the third step and looked back at her, Isabelle said, "Okay, but we're only going up there for as long as it takes to patch up Rick. It's every dog for herself, so when I say we go, we go."

Marnie yipped.

Rick's dad's place was just as I remembered it from my stay as a pup. I'd lived up here for two whole weeks after Rick picked me from a litter of two (by the way, he made the right choice — I have heard via the grapevine that my brother turned out to be a real putz). Before he handed me over to Isabelle for her birthday, this little aerie had been home sweet home and I'd loved it.

Dirty socks, crusty dishes, piles of newspapers, open books and rumpled clothing spread from here to there and back again greeted us. The man never threw away anything! To a nose as sensitive as mine, the place was a veritable cornucopia of heavenly scents.

Isabelle slipped off my leash, leaving me free to police the floor (popcorn under the sofa, half a cookie on the kitchen linoleum, whoopee!). Rick's dad got out all the medicinal things and sat glowering as Isabelle cleaned and patched Rick's face, hands and knees.

Don't get me wrong. I felt bad about what had happened to Rick. Of course, I'd had the situation in control when he grabbed my leash. He didn't know this, he was just trying to help. But look at him! The poor guy was bleeding and limping. Me? Nary a scratch!

People are just so fragile. It comes from a deficiency of fur. What fur people do have they cut, pluck, trim and shave. It's gross! No wonder they scratch and bruise so easily!

I digress.

The good side of what happened was that Isabelle had to get real close to Rick to clean his wounds and smear on antiseptic. I could tell he enjoyed her proximity. At least, I think I could tell. Okay, he winced a lot and complained occasionally and she sputtered and spewed about sissy men and stiff upper lips. I had no idea if he was enjoying it or not. Truth was, it didn't look terribly romantic.

Sigh. . . .

I desperately needed a nap — it had been hours since the last one — but I dared not close an eye lest I miss an opportunity to further my cause. I have to admit that I was currently out of ideas. I kept waiting for Rick to tell his father about his new girlfriend, hoping that might set off some sparks I could exploit, but even after the old man roused from his nap and Isabelle left the room to put the medical stuff away, Rick said nothing about what's-her-name. Instead, the two men held a kind of stilted conversation about sports. Before you knew it, we were on our way again.

You might think I would get discouraged. No way. If there's one thing we wire hair fox terriers don't do it's get discouraged. We improvise. So when we got close to the beach access trail, I whined and shivered and looked so all-around miserable that the next thing you knew, we were walking down to the beach.

Lots of memories on that beach. . . .

It had been a long time since Rick had stood on a windswept beach. In fact, the last time had been this exact beach and he'd been in the company of the same woman who currently walked beside him. Only then her arm had been looped cozily through his, her lips had been only a few inches away. She'd been his.

Now she walked a good foot from him,

contained and poised as she stripped off her sandals and walked barefoot in the sand. Though she was dressed in lightweight clothes, she wasn't even shivering from the cool wind. Apparently, she'd acclimated to the seaside weather since taking up full-time residence on the coast.

Marnie ran on ahead of them, barking like crazy, scaring flocks of gulls and sandpipers. Rick tried hard not to limp, but his right knee throbbed where Isabelle had wound bandages around and around while his newly ventilated slacks flapped in the breeze.

Nevertheless, he was glad Marnie had needed a potty break. This walk had the feeling of a proper ending. That's what he'd come to Seaport for: a new beginning with his father, a decent ending with Isabelle.

Not that the beginning of his reconciliation with his dad had been all that smooth. In typical fashion, the old man had refused to be led into a discussion of the past. He'd been relatively friendly, however, consenting to talk sports, so that was a beginning. Rick imagined the next time they met, they'd talk about boats and from there, they'd talk about everything under the sun but what had happened between them.

Life goes on.

That was okay. He'd wanted to mention Chloe today, but he hadn't dared. Despite his dad's typical gruff manner, that energetic climb up the steps had wiped the old man out. He'd sat in his big chair trying to catch his breath for way too long. The one ashtray was empty, but the old guy had never smoked indoors, not inside an old wooden building with a tinderbox of wooden boats directly underneath. Still, Rick had detected the sour smell of old smoke on his father's clothes — Isabelle was right; he was smoking.

Anyway, next time Rick visited, he would find a way to suggest a physical checkup *and* he'd mention Chloe. The time after that, he'd bring Chloe along.

Rick closed his eyes, trying to imagine that visit. He couldn't. He couldn't imagine Chloe in his dad's cluttered apartment; he couldn't imagine his dad accepting anyone but Isabelle as a potential daughter-in-law.

"Tell me about her," Isabelle said so softly it might have been the wind whispering.

Opening his eyes, he turned to face her. Her hand had already flown to cover her mouth as though mortified by her own request. Her big chocolate eyes looked anxious. And somehow, it didn't surprise him that she'd thought of Chloe at the same time he had.

"I'll tell you about her if you want," he said soothingly. "It's up to you."

Marnie had stopped running and was now trotting between them. It took Isabelle another hundred yards before she said, "Okay, tell me."

"Her name is Chloe Connors," he said.

Isabelle stared down at her feet and didn't say a word. They kept walking.

"Let's see. She has brown hair and eyes —"

"I saw her picture, I read the announcement," Isabelle interrupted. "Tell me *about* her."

"Well, she always looks nice." It was true, Chloe looked and moved like a model. "She likes to shop," he added. "She's full of energy, has tons of friends, excels in gourmet cooking and loves to travel."

As soon as the words were out he realized that Isabelle always looked slightly tousled, hated to shop, couldn't boil water, was very selective about her friends and was a confirmed homebody.

She wandered down toward the water, and he followed, anxious to hear what she might say next. Bending over to roll up her slacks, she stepped into the gentle surf that washed fine, black sand over her feet and up her legs. She caught her breath; in a flash, he recalled how cold that water was.

"Her father is a senior partner in your firm, isn't he?" Isabelle asked, turning to look at him from over her shoulder. Windblown strands of long dark hair blew across her eyes. "Connors, Henkle and Simms?"

Surprised she knew what firm he worked for, he answered with a nod.

"So how did you manage to woo his daughter?"

"I wooed no one," he said indignantly.

"You know what I mean. How did little old newcomer you hook up with the boss's daughter?"

"Actually, she came after me," he said modestly.

"That must have greased your ego. Couldn't be hurting your career, either."

"That's a rotten thing to say," he told her in a firm voice, though half of it was true. It *had* greased his ego . . . after Isabelle had shattered it.

Isabelle looked defiant for a moment, and then she whispered, "You're absolutely right. I'm sorry."

Water lapped at her shins. Rick looked from the water swirling around her feet and legs, up her slender body, lighting at last on her eyes. They looked unnaturally bright.

She bit her full lower lip.

In some kind of trance, he walked slowly into the water, shoes and all, staring at her face, at every lovely detail, filing her away in his mind.

"It's this beach," she said softly. "There are so many memories here. It's got me talking too much."

"I know," he said.

She licked the spray from her lips. By now, he was very close. She tilted her head back to look up at him the way she'd done a million times in the past. He felt his head lowering. He kept waiting for her to look away, to shrink back, to *do something* that would stop him.

Anything. Please.

But she didn't. Their mouths met with a tender thud. For an instant he thought to stop this kiss before it began, and then it was too late. He coaxed her lips open with the tip of his tongue, kissing her deeply until he no longer noticed the waves lapping around his shoes or the stinging spray against his abrasions. Her body seemed to melt against his.

Reason took that moment to reassert itself.

Better late than never.

By mutual consent, they separated.

Rick had never in his life felt as ashamed of himself as he did in that instant. He wasn't sure how to begin apologizing.

As if reading his thoughts, Isabelle said, "It was just a kiss, Rick. Don't look so guilty. I won't tell Chloe and I suggest you don't, either. It was just a goodbye kiss, inspired by this blasted beach. It didn't mean a thing."

To prove how little it meant to her, she laughed. Before he knew it, she'd taken off, running back the direction they had come. Marnie bounced along a few steps, then turned as though waiting for him to come, too.

He watched Isabelle's retreating form with a baffled expression.

And then a wave of relief washed over him at the same time a wave of a different sort caught him around the knees. He waded from the water, dripping wet, shoes squelching seawater.

"She's right," he announced as Marnie cocked her head and stared at him. Leaning down, the dog trotted back to sniff his outstretched fingers. She regarded him with her coal-black eyes as he rubbed her nose. "It was just a foolish kiss," he told Marnie. "It didn't mean a blasted thing."

He'd said goodbye to Isabelle; mission accomplished. She wasn't hurt, he wasn't hurt. It was over. He could drive home to Chloe, everything would go back to the way it was. The memory of Isabelle's lips would be just that: a memory.

Isabelle would be a memory.

Limping, he made his way up the beach.

By now you can see what I have to contend with.

He kisses her, she laughs?

It's over?

I don't think so . . .

Couldn't he tell how hollow that laugh was?

Couldn't she tell how out of character it was for him to wade into the water wearing a pricey pair of loafers just to kiss her goodbye?

Am I the only one with an ounce of brains?

So much for relying on the two of them to parlay my gentle hints into action. They're nice people, but they're kind of dense, don't you think? If I didn't do something quick, I was going to spend my golden years hanging out with Ignatz, the poodle.

By the way, I owe Ignatz one. It was his fault Mrs. Pughill complained about me to Isabelle. Sure, I'd barked a little when I heard Isabelle's car pulling into the drive after work; Rick had left a message and I wanted to make sure she got it in time to spruce herself up. But I hadn't barked all day long like Mrs. Pughill claimed. That had been her precious pooch; she'd accidentally locked him outside when she took her garbage out. I saw the whole thing from my vantage point through the kitchen window — it's in front of the sink and I was having a nice, refreshing drink of water from that drippy faucet. Anyway, while she watched those trashy talk shows all afternoon, her little darling yapped his head off.

And then he growled while Mrs. Pughill derided me in front of Isabelle and Rick!

He'd get his.

After Rick borrowed a towel and drove away, Isabelle scolded me for annoying Mrs. Pughill, for running off, for getting too sandy down at the beach. She was grouchy, so I let her blow off steam. Then her friend, Heather, called. I could hear Heather's wailing from clear across the room. Isabelle murmured a lot of comforting things but she never uttered one word about Rick. Drat. Maybe she'd confide in me when she got off the phone. I needed help. I'll admit I was stymied.

After the phone call ended, Isabelle microwaved herself a little dish of macaroni and cheese. She hardly ate a bite. Luckily, I was able to rescue the leftovers from the garbage can — it's a shame to waste such a tasty treat. Anyway, Isabelle was very quiet. She roamed from room to room, flipping on the television, turning it off, opening books, closing them, sitting down and standing up again. The girl was beginning to worry me.

I thought I knew what she needed. About the third time she found me sitting on the fuzzy pink bathroom rug, she took the hint and ran herself a bath. Not for me, mind you. I don't do baths unless I'm forced to. But that's another story.

Anyway, I like it when she fills the tub with smelly, bubbly water, turns down the lights, and lets me hang out while she soaks. We have some of our best "conversations" in that bathroom!

Sure enough, the hot water worked.

"Heather's marriage is a mystery to me," Isabelle mumbled as she leaned back in the tub. Lemon-scented steam rose all around her, fogging the mirror.

I didn't want to hear about Heather's marriage, but, as usual, I listened politely.

"This thing with John has gotten out of hand. All he wanted was to go to some boring seminar in Kansas City. All he wanted was some 'space,' whatever that is. Why was she so hurt when he didn't invite her to go with him? And then, once he discovered it meant so much to her, why didn't he just take her? Aren't people supposed to give and take in a marriage? Now she's all alone and he's living at his brother's house and he doesn't even know he's going to have a baby in a few months."

She fell silent, so I yipped to encourage her to keep talking, hoping she'd eventually get around to something more pertinent than Heather. Isabelle peered at me from over the lip of the tub and added, "Get this. Right after school is out, she wants me to come to Portland to help her cater some big party for some girl who lives in her building! Can't you just see me trying to make idle chitchat with a room full of strangers? What in the world would I say to them? And what would I cook? Microwave popcorn? Toast? What is Heather thinking? I told her I'd consider it, but honestly, her pregnancy is making her crazy. And I don't need the money, not if I budget carefully. We can have the whole summer off, you and me, to . . . well, we'll think of something fun to do, won't we, sweetie? We'll go camping, maybe. Honestly."

With that, she plunged under the water and came up sputtering. "As if I'd want to go to Portland," she added, lathering her hair like a woman possessed. "I never want to go there again, not ever."

She dove back under the water.

I knew why she didn't want to go to Portland

— for the very same reason I wanted her to go.

Now what?

Chapter Five

Isabelle drove home from work on the last day of school with a serious case of melancholy. Along with the relief that came at the end of the year was the sadness that her kids would all move along to a new teacher the coming fall. This was only her third year teaching. She had a soft spot in her heart for each and every one of her students.

Even the kid with the trumpet.

Anyway, she wanted all of them to go on and flourish, but it kind of hurt to be left behind.

For a second, she reconsidered Heather's catering proposal. Besides the fact that she couldn't cook and was dismal with groups of adults, what was to keep her from giving it a try? It would fill a few weeks, it would earn her a little extra cash, it would give her the chance to talk sense into Heather and it would be exciting to live in Portland.

"No way," she said, slamming her hand

against the steering wheel.

In her head, Portland meant Rick. She didn't want to see Rick again. Not ever.

Instead, she would stay home and putter. She would figure out a way to keep Marnie inside the backyard fence. She would drive down the coast and camp out for a week. She'd visit Rick's dad and perhaps work on getting him to go in for a checkup. She would plant a few flowers, read a few books, rent a few movies and maybe, maybe, even go out on a few dates!

She arrived home to find Mrs. Pughill watering the roses. She waved at her landlady who glared in return, tried to pat Ignatz who growled in response, and let herself into her half of the duplex. At least Mrs. Pughill hadn't regaled her with horror stories about Marnie's bad behavior.

What she saw when she stepped inside caused her to close the door quickly behind her lest Mrs. Pughill should wander over and peer inside. In fact, she quickly crossed to the front window and closed the drapes as well.

She couldn't breathe!

She'd be evicted!

"How could you?" she cried at last. "Marnie, how could you?"

Marnie, who had been lying as though

exhausted, sat up and yawned. She managed to look proud of the havoc she'd wreaked in the seven and a half hours Isabelle had been at work.

The beige carpeting in the duplex had been installed just days before Mrs. Pughill rented the place to Isabelle. This fact had been repeatedly drilled into Isabelle's head in ways such as, "Wipe your feet so that you don't track mud onto the new carpeting," and "Make sure that dog of yours doesn't piddle on my expensive new rug!" What Mrs. Pughill lacked in subtlety, she made up for with repetition.

Marnie had not tracked or piddled on the carpet. Instead, she'd torn it up!

Starting at the floor-mounted heater vent and working her way out toward the living room, she'd apparently dug and clawed her way through carpet and padding until the resulting excavation site was now approximately the size and shape of a hula hoop. The dog was all tuckered out. Beige fibers hung from her mouth. Bits of blue-flecked carpet padding were caught in her whiskers.

Isabelle crossed the room and fell to her knees. For one wild moment, she desperately tried to pat everything back into place.

With a sigh, she plopped onto her rear and surveyed the room. From the bedroom, past the vent and on to the front door, a distance of at least twelve feet, the carpet was one continuous expanse. In fact, there were no seams for the whole twelve-by-fourteen-foot room. No way to mend the hole. No way to hide it, no way to do anything but fess up and incur the wrath of Bertha Pughill!

"How could you?" Isabelle said again.

Marnie cocked her head as though trying to understand Isabelle's obvious distress. She sneezed. She licked Isabelle's arm and whined softly.

"Is that supposed to be an apology?" Isabelle snapped as she dislodged the long synthetic fibers from the dog's teeth and brushed away the spongy bits of padding. " 'Cause if it is, it isn't enough. How am I going to afford to fix this before Mrs. Pughill gets wind of what you've done? She'll kick us out of here, and she'll have every right to keep every penny of my deposit. I won't have enough left to rent you a doghouse, let alone me a decent place to live."

Isabelle delved in her shoulder bag. Finding her bankbook, she scanned the savings column.

"Two hundred and eight-eight dollars and fifty-four cents," she said aloud. "I'm going to have to get a summer job." There was only one summer job she could think of.

Marnie woofed.

Isabelle stared at her.

"You do realize you can't come to Portland with me," she said at last. "Can you imagine Heather allowing you to stay in her apartment? What would the management say? What would the health inspector say? She runs her catering business out of that place. Oh, no, my dear little four-footed friend. You are going to have to go to a kennel. It's kind of like dog jail. Bars. No snacks. No cozy bath mat. No dripping faucets for fresh water. You'll have to drink out of a bowl like an ordinary dog. Ha!"

Marnie began panting, though if it was in response to Isabelle's threats or to overexertion brought on by hours of strenuous labor, it was impossible to tell.

"I'm going to have to go to Portland," Isabelle said aloud, just to get used to the idea. "Maybe Rick will come back to visit Heather's building again. Maybe his fiancée lives in the same building. Maybe we'll run into each other and make inane conversation in the elevator."

That was a dreadful thought. There had to be another way. She did a little mental math. It was too late to sign up for teaching summer school. She might be able to get some menial job in town, but at minimum wages, she'd spend the whole summer working from morning to night just to make enough to buy the carpet. The catering job would pay well enough that she could dig herself out of this mess within a month. That would leave her another month before school started again. If she could tolerate the possibility of running into Rick, she could still salvage something of her summer.

"Why should I allow Rick to dictate where I go and what I do?" she demanded of Marnie.

Marnie, looking dejected, didn't respond. She did, however, sneeze.

First of all, have you ever had carpet fibers stuck between your teeth or had that foamy padding stuff up your nose? Keep in mind my nose is almost four inches long! Very unpleasant. . . .

Secondly, me stay at a kennel? I don't think so. Kennels are for Labrador retrievers and German shepherds, big dogs. Not nice little cute dogs like me. No way.

Unless your name is Ignatz. If your name is Ignatz, you belong at a kennel. Period.

Had I outsmarted myself?

Isabelle was going to Portland without me!

■ ■ ■ ■

In the end, Isabelle took Marnie with her. The kennels all cost an arm and a leg. The only friend she knew who liked dogs well enough to take Marnie for a month was traveling in Canada. Rick's father offered, but she knew Carl Manning would have a hard time keeping track of Marnie. The building in which he built boats was often open to the boatyard, which was often open to the street. Marnie had already proven how clever she was when it came to traffic by coming close to getting herself, and Rick, run over.

Speaking of Rick, why couldn't he help out? Rick was in Portland, he had to have a pretty nice apartment, it was his turn to give Marnie a temporary home!

Heather had been so overjoyed that Isabelle had changed her mind about taking the job that she'd agreed Marnie could stay in the guest room until Isabelle contacted Rick. Isabelle had told Mrs. Pughill she was going off to the city for a while, turned off the furnace and covered the hole in the carpet with a big area rug that kind of dipped in the middle. The rug looked a trifle odd sitting out there all by its lonesome, but if Mrs. Pughill should go inside the apartment while Isabelle was gone, at least she wouldn't see the damage.

Unless she lifted the rug.

After that, Isabelle took her floor measurement and a carpet sample to three different stores until she found one who recognized the ruined rug and was willing to order enough to re-do her living room. She got a price quote that made her gulp, ordered the carpet and used her entire savings as a deposit.

All that was left to do was buy a new pair of black pants and a white blouse to wear when acting as Heather's assistant, pack a bag for herself and the essentials for Marnie and lock the door behind her. Marnie bounced into the car as though they were off on an adventure.

Ha!

Isabelle had expected to find Heather a dejected mess. She'd expected red-rimmed eyes, a glazed expression, a voice tinged with tears. In short, she'd expected the same woman she'd visited the Sunday before, the same woman who had sobbed on the phone the day before, the same woman who had pleaded with Isabelle to drop everything and come "save" her.

What she found was a barefoot Heather wearing a red apron over short denim coveralls. She shoved a tiny shrimp covered bite of cucumber at Isabelle as she took Isabelle's suitcase and set it aside.

"Tell me what you think," Heather said as she closed the front door behind Isabelle. "I used a sprig of dill. Nice, huh? Come on into the kitchen. I'm making sample hors d'oeuvres for an engagement party I'm catering two weeks from now. Trying out new recipes, you know? Getting some ready for the party planner who is stopping by tomorrow night. John usually helps, but John is in Kansas City, as you well know. Or maybe he's back at his brother's house by now. Who knows? Who cares? Come on, only don't bring Marnie because she can't come into the kitchen, not ever. Close the door on her. If the health inspector caught her in there, it would mean big trouble."

This speech was delivered as Heather moved across the pale blue carpet of her living room. To Isabelle, this room reflected Heather's currently absent husband. Cool colors, refined taste, elegant but kind of remote. Watercolors on the walls, satin pillows on the sofa, arrangements of silk flowers on the tables.

She looked into the kitchen where the

ambience changed right along with the color scheme.

Riotous oranges, yellows and reds ruled the day in the kitchen. Posters of food, both raw and cooked, stacked in pyramids and arranged like suspects in a police lineup, covered the walls. Every kind of appliance in the world seemed to be represented, half of them looking as though they'd recently been pressed into service.

With a stern look at Marnie and the command to stay, Isabelle let the door swing shut behind her. She nudged it open again. Marnie hadn't moved, but there was a shifty look in her eyes that made Isabelle loop her leash over a closet doorknob, just to be on the safe side. The dog had been acting kind of odd lately.

Back in the kitchen, every surface was covered with plates and dishes of food. Platters heaped with raw vegetables. Crostini cooling on racks, a rainbow assortment of sauces, each tucked into a colorful container. Skewers of beef and chicken ready to grill, vegetables and fruit as fresh as dew. It all looked beautiful. Isabelle's stomach growled.

"Try the fennel-encrusted smoked salmon," Heather said as she washed her hands.

Isabelle popped a morsel in her mouth. "Yum," she said, licking her lips as she perched on a stool. "Heather, who in the world is going to eat all this?"

Heather waved a hand. "Well, some of it you and I can eat for dinner, some is for the brunch we're catering tomorrow, and some is for the party planner who is coming by tomorrow night to taste a few samples so he can choose the menu for that engagement party I told you about. I'll freeze the leftovers."

Isabelle looked at her friend, who was busily pouring cream into a copper bowl. "Are you okay?" she asked.

"Never better," Heather chirped.

"I thought pregnant women couldn't be around food. I thought it made them nauseous."

"Not me. I have a cast-iron stomach."

"But —"

"I'm fine," Heather said sternly. A tall woman with a mane of flaming red hair currently pinned on top of her head, Heather did look well. She always reminded Isabelle of an Irish setter, not only because of her rosy coloring, but also because she moved with the long-legged gait associated with that breed.

A few months before, John had convinced

Heather to let her catering partner go and announced he'd be helping her instead. It meant they would have more time together, John had explained. Heather had admitted to being flattered, but now that John had flown the coop, it meant Heather had no backup. "Why don't you whip up a lime aioli sauce for the crab cakes I'm planning for the brunch?" Heather said, whisking the cream into soft clouds.

"A what?" Isabelle said, almost choking on a slice of red pepper.

"Lime aioli?"

"I wouldn't know lime aioli from ketchup. Heather, you haven't forgotten I don't cook, have you?"

"Oh. Of course not," Heather said.

"I'll do whatever you want, but you'll have to give me explicit instructions. I can follow a recipe if it's not too complicated."

"Can you make mayonnaise?"

"I can open a jar. You mean you actually make it yourself?"

"Of course I do."

"I had no idea anyone actually made mayonnaise. I thought it was one of those things that just . . . happens."

"For heaven's sake, Isabelle, it's just eggs and oil —"

"Heather, I'm sorry —"

A scratching at the kitchen door reminded them both that Marnie needed attending to. Heather said, "It's not your fault. Listen, why don't you call Rick to come get your dog? I'm fine in here for now."

Isabelle nodded. She was beginning to wonder how in the world she could honestly earn enough to fix her carpet. What had made her think she could cook, recipe or no recipe? And to top it off, Heather didn't seem to need any emotional support whatsoever! One hand on the door, Isabelle turned back to Heather. "What happened to you? Last night you were crying in my ear, and today you look and act like nothing is wrong."

"I just decided I'd cried enough over John. I have to consider the health of my baby." She patted her flat stomach and added, "John is a selfish bore. He's an accountant for goodness sake! I don't need him." She looked away quickly but not before Isabelle saw tears sparkle in her eyes.

"I'll call Rick," Isabelle said.

"You need me to what?" Rick said a few moments later.

"I need you to keep Marnie for a few weeks."

"Marnie? Here?"

"I'm helping a friend who runs a commercial kitchen out of her apartment. It would just be easier if you took the dog for a month or so."

"*You're* helping a caterer?" he said, a trace of amusement in his voice. Boy, did that tone bring back memories! He'd loved to tease her and she'd loved to tease him back. For a second, she found a smile stealing across her face; she was about to remind him of the time she'd tried to make s'mores by putting the chocolate pieces on the outside of the graham crackers. She let the story and the smile fade away without acknowledgment and barked, "Just come get this blasted dog!"

"I'm sorry, Isabelle," Rick said. "I can't."

In a low voice, she said, "I've never asked a favor of you, Rick. You bought me this little tyrant, the least you can do is help me out when I'm in a jam."

"I can't," he said. "I'm sorry. My life is different than it used to be. I don't have the space or the time to care for a demanding dog. Now, if there's nothing else, I'm running late."

Banging down the receiver, Isabelle fumed for a few moments. Marnie, leash still looped over the doorknob, stared at her, head tilted to one side, shiny black eyes focused on Isabelle's face.

"He can't take you," she said.

Marnie woofed.

Isabelle knelt down and undid the little dog's leash, running a hand over her wiry coat. "What are we doing here?" she whispered near one fawn-colored ear. "I want to go home."

Lowering her head, Marnie scooted along the rug, rubbing the left side of her face against the blue carpet, falling over on her side and rolling over and over like a little kid in a bed of clover. Another memory assaulted Isabelle. Summertime, her and Rick, Marnie still a puppy. They'd driven up into the mountains and picnicked near a creek. After lunch, they'd all three rolled around on the grassy banks. Marnie had fallen asleep as she and Rick lost themselves in each other. . . .

"I'm sorry he doesn't want you," she said, patting Marnie's pink tummy. "Don't worry, we'll think of something."

That evening, Isabelle carefully watched Heather make mayonnaise. Amazing! She then watched Heather use the mayonnaise to make lime aioli. Then Heather whipped up a recipe of crab cakes while Isabelle was in charge of charring a dozen green chilies on the indoor grill.

The next morning, Isabelle was trusted to take fresh corn off the cob for corn bread. After that, as Heather made some kind of chili-egg dish, Isabelle mangled a slew of tomatoes for salsa. She diced coriander. She chopped an onion. She listened as Heather patiently explained how she'd diced and chopped all wrong, and biting her lip, did it over again.

She learned how to pack the hot foods separate from the cold foods, how to use the freight elevator to get everything down to the underground garage and into Heather's specially equipped van, how to set things up once they were at the hostess's house. She was better at these things than the actual cooking. She learned how to serve, smile, nod and defer all questions to Heather. Some of that she excelled at; every decent kindergarten teacher knows how to smile and nod through almost anything.

Later, she moved on to cleaning-up duties, transporting everything back to Heather's apartment, storing the few leftovers and loading the dishwasher.

She was pooped and it wasn't even three o'clock in the afternoon yet.

"This is hard work," Isabelle said as she tore off the little bow tie Heather had insisted she wear at the brunch. Along with the crisp white blouse and the tailored black trousers, the bow tie made Isabelle feel like an extra in an old Charlie Chaplin movie. All she needed was a mustache. To her horror, Heather opened the cupboard and began taking out more ingredients.

"Be sure you put that tie back on before Freddy Randy gets here," Heather said.

"Tell me you're not cooking again," Isabelle moaned. "And who in the heck is Freddy Randy?"

Cutting the top third off a loaf of Italian bread, Heather said, "He's the party planner who's due here in three hours to taste the sample hors d'oeuvres for that engagement party. I told you about this."

"Don't you want to put your feet up for a few minutes or . . . something?"

"I can't," Heather said, her hands now tearing the center out of the loaf, chunks of bread flying onto a cookie sheet. She spritzed them with olive oil as she added, "John was supposed to help me with this party. Freddy Randy said the bride is adamant, she wants an hors d'oeuvres party. I'm good with entrées and desserts, but John really knows his appetizers. When we agreed to the party format, John was going to do half the work. Now I have to do it all myself."

Isabelle stood there for a second, kind of stunned into silence. What had she been doing all day if not helping?

Heather suddenly seemed to realize what she'd said, and the way in which she'd said it. She had the grace to look embarrassed. "I'm sorry, Isabelle," she mumbled as she slid the cookie sheet into the oven. Isabelle didn't have the slightest idea why Heather was fussing with bread. "You've been a huge help. I couldn't have done the brunch without you."

"It's okay," Isabelle said. "I know what you mean. I'm not much help in the food preparation department."

"You're doing fine. Why don't you go take care of Marnie while I toast these oversize croutons? I'll rub them with a cut garlic clove when they're hot out of the oven. Oh, and when you get back, would you pipe wasabi cream cheese onto endive leaves?"

"Uh, sure," Isabelle said, hoping by now that Heather knew she needed to create the wasabi whatever herself. "What do we need oversize croutons for?" Isabelle ventured.

"Our dinner. I'm craving a tossed salad with garlic croutons. We'll eat after Freddy leaves. I don't think I can face another dinner of hors d'oeuvres. By the way, be sure you keep Marnie locked in the back bedroom. All I need is Freddy telling people I have a dog running through my place. Talk about discouraging business."

"I'm sorry Rick wouldn't take Marnie," Isabelle said for what felt like the fortieth time.

"You can't depend on a man," Heather said from her new anti-male pulpit. "Don't worry about it," she added with a smile.

"I'll take Marnie on a quick walk and feed her dinner early," Isabelle said. "Her stomach more or less rules her life. She'll be happy to nap later if I take care of her now. Then I'll come back here and help you get ready for Freddy Randy. Is that his real name?"

"I think so."

Isabelle happily escaped the kitchen. How Heather could start cooking again so soon after cleaning up after the last venture was beyond her. As for dinner . . . homemade croutons? Couldn't they just microwave something? If Heather's errant husband thought weekends spent this way were fun, Heather needed to get him back because he truly was a treasure. It suddenly occurred to Isabelle that the "space" John kept talking about might simply be his way of trying to tell Heather that he was tired of working harder on the weekends than he did at the office Monday through Friday — even though it was his idea to help out in the first place. Heather was right, men couldn't be trusted.

Meanwhile, the reason Isabelle was currently stuck in Portland cooking away her summer sat in the spare room, square in the middle of the canopied bed, legs straight out in front of her, ears perky, eyes bright, looking like a canine sphinx.

Isabelle had tried and tried to convince the dog to stay off the bedspread but it was no use. Marnie seldom did anything Marnie didn't want to do, especially if no one was watching. In defeat, Isabelle had spread a sweater atop the bed for the dog to sit on.

Of course, Marnie wasn't sitting on the sweater.

She preferred the delicate eyelet spread.

Tossing the stupid bow tie on the dresser, Isabelle sat down next to Marnie and clipped on the leash in preparation for their clandestine walk. They'd use the stairs and the fire exit to circumnavigate the building management.

"You'll be a good girl, tonight, won't you?" she crooned as she slipped her little pal a leftover crab cake she'd pocketed during cleanup.

Marnie yipped once.
Did once mean *yes* or did once mean *no?*
Who knew?

CHAPTER SIX

Marnie here. I did not connive my way to Portland to spend my life wasting away in Heather's spare bedroom! Nevertheless, the day hadn't been a complete waste. Denied activity, I'd concentrated very hard between naps, telepathically communicating with both Isabelle's and Rick's subconscious.

To Isabelle, I'd sent the message: bring me a snack! Hence the crab cake, a tasty little tidbit that went down in one dainty gulp! Honestly, the smells wafting through the apartment were outrageous.

My biggest priority was finding a way out of the bedroom with no one the wiser. The door handle was the lever kind and I figured a jump or two would unlatch it. I hadn't tried it yet because I couldn't figure out how to close the door from the other side. No reason to alert Isabelle as to my intentions. I mean, once she figured out I could open that door, she'd tie me to the bedpost and that really would cramp my style when it came time to . . . well, time to do something.

Anyway, to Rick I'd sent the message: Come get me. I needed a little time to work on the man at close range. Okay, I admit it threw me for a loop when Rick refused Isabelle's request to take me in for a few weeks. For a moment or two, I even felt a slight twinge somewhere around my heart, but as I believe I've stated before: wire fox terriers don't get discouraged, they get creative.

Hence the deep thoughts.

However, since the psychic element of my two-part plan wasn't half as much fun to implement as taking action, I knew I had to keep alert and look for any and all possibilities to make things happen.

And by the way, one yip means yes unless the dog doing the yipping changes her mind mid-yip and then it means no. Or vice versa.

Freddy Randy was a man of about thirty-five. It looked as though he'd tried to compensate for the fact that he was prematurely balding by growing a ponytail in the back. He spoke fast, was prone to wide gestures, and always seemed to be on the edge of a nervous giggle.

Isabelle, wearing the bow tie again, schlepped tray after tray of elegant little hors d'oeuvres between the kitchen and the table in the dining alcove. Freddy looked each morsel over as though it was a rare gem being readied for display in a museum. He spoke often into a very small tape recorder as Heather described each ingredient she'd used to create her mini-masterpieces.

Isabelle tuned them both out. She smiled as she schlepped, but her mind was far away. She wondered what kind of weather Seaport was enjoying; she'd bet it was warm, with a cool breeze blowing from the northwest. She wondered if Mrs. Pughill had trespassed into Isabelle's side of the duplex yet. The woman was an incurable snoop. She wondered how she was going to survive another month of this catering schedule, though it would probably relax some during the week.

When the doorbell rang, she came close to dropping a basket of crostini. Freddy, who had retreated to the sofa, jumped to his feet. Isabelle had just a second to wonder why Freddy had settled down on the sofa instead of staying near the table, nibbling the goodies set out for his perusal.

"I'll get it," Freddy said, already halfway across the room. "Undoubtedly it's my happy little couple," he called. "*She's* very involved with the party planning," he added with a titter, glancing over his shoulder as he imparted this last bit of information. The look on his face and the tone of his voice left no doubt how obnoxious Freddy Randy found an interfering bride-to-be.

"I'm sorry," Heather whispered, sidling close to Isabelle. "I never heard the groom's name mentioned and the bride's name didn't mean a thing to me. I see her in the elevator off and on, and she saw my brochure in the lobby . . . Listen, if I'd read the newspaper more carefully I would have recognized her name when Freddy Randy told me who she was, but I didn't, I was too upset about John."

Jungle drums began beating in Isabelle's head as she mumbled, "What?"

Freddy opened the door. His welcoming laugh rang through the room.

"I must say you're taking this well," Heather added. "I about fell off my chair when Freddy told me they were coming, but you didn't even react."

"I . . . I wasn't paying attention," Isabelle stammered. "Who's coming? What are you talking about?"

But by then, Freddy had ushered the happy couple into the room and what Heather was talking about became crystal clear.

The woman was a blur. The man looked a lot like Rick for the excellent reason that he *was* Rick.

He said, "Isabelle?"

Isabelle, who felt all the blood drain from her face, said, "Hello, Rick."

Heather aborted a painfully long pause by saying, "Hey, Rick, remember me?"

With what seemed an effort, Rick looked away from Isabelle. Her knees felt weak. For a second there, his gaze had been as gravitational as the earth's pull on the moon.

"Heather!" Glancing down at his intended, he said, "Our caterer is Heather Stewart?"

"Not Heather Stewart, Heather McGee."

"I'm married," Heather said, with only a slight pause between the two uttered words. She reached out a hand, but Rick ignored it and folded her in a hug.

"It's great to see you," he said. "It's been ages." He turned back to his fiancée and added, "Heather and I went to college together."

Heather was looking at Rick closely, scrutinizing his face. "What happened to you? You look like you lost a fight with a mountain lion!"

"He was trying to stop an animal from getting run over and ended up in the street himself," Rick's companion gushed. "Daddy and I both said he should sue the dog's owner or the city itself for improper animal control or faulty sidewalks, but Rick won't hear of it."

Rick glanced surreptitiously at Isabelle, then quickly away. Was he afraid she'd blow his cover and tell everyone that it was *her* misbehaved dog that was responsible for almost getting him killed? Not likely, though it was interesting which details Rick had chosen to tell Chloe . . . and which he hadn't.

"Thank heavens it'll be all better before our engagement party," his fiancée said. "I'd hate for him to look like this in the pictures."

Chloe was shorter and thinner than Isabelle. Her sleek dark hair was pulled into a knot at the back of her head. Her makeup, from her glossy pink lips to the taupe eye shadow that emphasized her large, dark eyes, was applied to perfection. She wore money in the form of a thousand-dollar suit and a silk scarf that fluttered behind her when she moved, both done in pure bridal white. Presently, she was glued to Rick, her arm looped through his, snuggled close to his side, all soft and perfumed and cooing.

Isabelle felt ridiculous in her Charlie Chaplin outfit. She and Heather looked as though they were getting ready to audition for a vaudeville act.

"And how about *this one?*" Chloe said. Her voice had a slightly acidic quality to it, but that might have been because she'd tuned into the tension in the room.

With a jolt, Isabelle realized *this one,* meant her.

Rick said, "I met Isabelle in college, too. Isabelle Winters, meet Chloe Connors."

"Isabelle *Winters,*" Chloe repeated, lightbulbs obviously going off in her head. For some reason, the thought that Rick had shared his memories of her and their relationship with Chloe Connors made Isabelle furious. "So, this is *that* Isabelle," Chloe said.

Rick nodded, looking from Chloe to Isabelle and back again.

"Everywhere we go, from the grocery store to the cleaners, Rick runs into someone he knows!" Chloe said, reaching up to pat his cheek. "Daddy says knowing so many working people is good for business, but for heaven's sake, who would have dreamed he once dallied with a caterer?"

Dallied?

Dallied!

"Actually, I'm not a caterer, I'm a teacher," Isabelle said. "I'm here just to help my friend."

Heather looked alarmed and Isabelle realized that perhaps she shouldn't have risen to the bait and admitted she wasn't a caterer.

Freddy laughed nervously as he grabbed Chloe's arm and guided her toward the table, babbling on about the merits of this canapé over that one. Heather hurried along after them. That left Rick and Isabelle standing awkwardly by the front door.

"So Heather is the caterer friend you're helping this summer," Rick said in a voice barely over a whisper.

"So that's the boss's daughter," Isabelle growled softly.

Rick said, "Isabelle," in a warning way.

"She's a snob! Where does she get off saying you *dallied* with me?"

"She's under a lot of pressure," he said. "Planning a wedding is hard work."

"But *dallied?* It's such a silly word!"

"Listen, how would you like to meet your fiancée's last girlfriend while sampling canapés for your own engagement party? Cut her some slack."

"What are you even doing here?" Isabelle demanded. "You have a party planner. Go home and let Freddy Randy do his job."

"Chloe wants to be part of every decision," he said.

"Heaven forbid you have square crackers instead of round."

"Speaking of going home where you belong, Isabelle, why don't you?"

"Because the dog you gave me has created a little bit of a financial . . . strain . . . on my budget. In other words, Mr. Hotshot lawyer, I need the job."

"I'll loan you what you need. Go home."

"As if I'd borrow money from you," Isabelle scoffed.

A knot formed in Rick's scraped but healing jaw. "Why are you being so hostile?"

She met his gaze and stared into his eyes. They were as dark as a moonless night, and currently filled with emotion. Irritation, probably, because she was attacking his beloved.

And it struck Isabelle like a ton of bricks. She still had unresolved feelings for this guy. Thanks to that tiny interlude on the beach, the feel of his lips against hers was brand spanking new instead of old and moldering away in the back of her subconscious where it belonged.

Did she want him back?

No, that ship had sailed; they were too different. She couldn't stand being around Rick, the lawyer. But did she want to watch him romance another woman?

Absolutely not.

No way.

But this wasn't the time or place to act surly. She was letting her own insecurities and jealousies jeopardize Heather's business. She said, "I'm sorry."

He started to touch her arm and then apparently thought better of it. "I know Chloe can be a little . . . difficult."

"As in spoiled rotten?"

"Isabelle. Please."

"I know, I know. I'm sorry."

Chloe called from the other end of the room. "Honey? Are you going to come taste these little things or not?"

With a final warning scowl, Rick moved off toward his fiancée and the table o' goodies.

Isabelle considered her options. She could hide in the kitchen; she could hide in the guest room; she could stand there like a third wheel. And then she thought about Marnie and wondered what would happen when the little dog recognized Rick's voice. She'd bark like crazy, that's what would happen, and poor Heather would come unglued.

Isabelle skirted the perimeter of the room to the small hallway. She'd spend the next hour with her dog. Heather didn't really need any more help until after Rick and Chloe left, when Isabelle could make up for the fact that her presence was a business distraction by hand-washing Heather's handmade serving dishes.

The bedroom door was open!

Isabelle rushed inside, hoping she'd find Marnie asleep on the eyelet spread if not on the sweater. No dog.

How had the little rascal escaped this room?

How long had she been free?

Why hadn't Isabelle seen her lurking about the apartment?

Where was Marnie and what was she up to?

Pithy Observation:

Most people think dogs will eat anything and in all fairness, most of the time they are right. The measure of a dog comes not in what she will eat when there are no options, but in what she will choose to eat when there are.

Isabelle glanced into the dining alcove. The table was still covered with platters sporting wilted lettuce leaves, abandoned cherry tomatoes and sprigs of parsley, i.e., mostly garnishes. Heather's tidbits had been all but demolished. Thankfully, Marnie was not standing in the middle of the table and Isabelle took a grateful breath.

She walked into the living room, expecting to find Marnie plastered to Rick. Instead, four sets of eyes glanced up to greet her. Rick and Chloe were sitting side by side on the sofa, Freddy Randy was sitting on the ottoman, apparently explaining something, his hands moving in broad arcs. Heather sat alone in a club chair off to the side.

No dog.

That left Heather's bedroom, the bathroom and the kitchen.

The kitchen!

"What's wrong, Isabelle?" Heather asked, her voice curiously flat.

Isabelle began edging her way toward the kitchen. From this side, the hinged door that swung open with a good thump from a hip if need be, appeared firmly closed. "Ah, nothing," she said.

With a dull inflection that caught Isabelle's attention, Heather added, "Chloe and Rick have decided on a raw seafood bar for their party. Isn't that . . . exciting?"

Isabelle paused midstep. "A raw seafood bar?" Rick was allergic to most seafood; it seemed an odd choice.

In a singsong voice, Freddy Randy listed, "Oysters, jumbo shrimp, crab claws, clams, mussels —"

"Rick's dad is a man of the sea," Chloe said imperiously. "We know he'll appreciate a seafood bar. Freddy says it will be an icebreaker. Rick is thrilled."

To Isabelle's eyes, Rick didn't appear to be particularly thrilled, but then, what did she know about this new, improved, engaged-to-be-married Rick? Not much. She struggled not to smile as she imagined Carl Manning in his black denim pants and red suspenders eating raw oysters while his only son broke out in hives!

Chloe added, "But I have to admit the most compelling reason to go seafood is *my* father. Daddy just loves seafood, especially Beluga caviar."

"Funny, *my* daddy is a Polish sausage kind of guy," Isabelle said, immediately regretting her flippancy. It wasn't Rick's impatient sigh or Randy's nervous laugh that got to her; it was Heather's downcast eyes.

"Why am I not surprised?" Chloe said icily.

Isabelle, remembering her mission, once again started backing toward the kitchen. "Well, a raw seafood bar sounds . . . dandy.

If you'll just excuse me . . ."

At that instant, the kitchen door bounced open on its hinges, banging against the dining area wall with enough force to catch the attention of everyone in the room if not everyone on the fourth floor of the building. Except Heather, who didn't even look up.

Out through the door pranced Marnie, the entire hollowed out loaf of bread clutched between her jaws, jutting out on either side of her snout by a good eight inches. The dog quickly sidestepped Isabelle and flew across the room, landing with a graceful leap on Chloe's lap.

Gasping, Chloe pushed the dog away and jumped to her feet.

Marnie stood, bread still in place, tail fiercely wagging.

"What in the world is that thing?" screeched Chloe. "Rick, what's it doing here? Get rid of it!"

Rick got to his feet, and leaning over, took the bread from Marnie and handed it to Isabelle. He then scooped Marnie into his arms. His lips struggled with a smile as he regarded the dog.

"*This* is Marnie," he said. "She's a wire hair fox terrier."

"But where . . . where did she come

from?" Chloe sputtered.

"I gave her to Isabelle for her birthday a few years ago. She's really a little sweetheart." With that, he nuzzled Marnie's curly head. "You're a good girl, aren't you, lamb chop? Just a trifle mischievous." This earned him a quick lick on his hand.

Isabelle's heart kind of melted. This was the Rick she'd known and loved; the man who rose to the defense of a silly dog and accepted a lick or two in gratitude; the man who knew when something was serious and when something wasn't; the man who recognized humor in the bizarre.

For one instant, the room kind of blurred and Isabelle was back at the beach, Rick wading through the surf, a mesmerizing look in his eye. She could almost feel the warmth of his body as he came closer, the cool mist on her face, hear the roar of the waves, the pounding of her heart . . .

"But it's a dog!" Freddy said, and the room came back into sharp focus.

"Yes," Rick agreed. "It's a dog."

Isabelle set aside the bread and stretched out her arms; Rick handed over Marnie.

"This is unconscionable!" Freddy insisted. "That animal came from the . . . the kitchen!"

"Isn't that against the law?" Chloe

squealed.

This comment finally snapped Heather out of her stupor. "The kitchen? She came from the kitchen? No, that's impossible."

"I assure you," Freddy said, "the dog did come from the kitchen."

Heather looked at Isabelle. Isabelle nodded. "I'm sorry. I don't know how she got out of the bedroom. I'll go buy one of those little kennels things with a big lock . . ."

"There are strict health codes," Freddy interrupted. "Violators can lose their license —"

"How will the health department hear about this little incident?" Isabelle said, fighting to keep her voice calm. "Marnie doesn't live here, she's just visiting. This won't ever happen again."

"I'm sure I won't know if it does or not," Chloe said, leveling her gaze at Isabelle. "I can't see giving my business to a catering outfit with such a laissez-faire attitude when it comes to allowing animals in the kitchen. Daddy would never approve."

Isabelle bit back a quick retort.

Heather said, "Ms. Connors, please. The dog doesn't even live here. Not really."

"Wait a second," Isabelle said, addressing Chloe. "You aren't threatening to pull your party from Heather, are you?"

Chloe's cheeks blushed a pretty pink as she defiantly started to nod.

Rick chose that moment to speak. "Of course we're not."

His comment earned him a frown from Chloe.

"Think about it," he told her in a soft voice that made every hair on Isabelle's head kind of tingle. "Nothing has changed. You said the hors d'oeuvres were delicious so obviously, you enjoy Heather's cooking. Now she's agreed to do the seafood thing you want. I'm sure Isabelle will find a different place for Marnie by tomorrow. The dog isn't an issue."

"He's right," Isabelle said. "She isn't an issue. As a matter of fact, Rick will take Marnie home with him right now, won't you Rick?"

He stared at her a moment that stretched on into infinity. Isabelle was aware of the clock ticking on the faux mantel, of Heather's suppressed breath, of Chloe's gnashing teeth, of Freddy Randy's suspended titter.

Rick finally said, "Sure. I'll take her."

The titter exploded, the breath expelled, the teeth kept gnashing. Almost as though the dog understood the conversation, she wiggled in Isabelle's arms, trying to get back to Rick.

"But you can't!" Chloe gasped. "Mr. Charles —"

"Mr. Charles will be fine," Rick said, as Marnie managed to squirm into his arms. "Don't worry about it, honey. It'll work. Trust me," he said.

"So everything is okay?" Freddy Randy said, clapping his hands together. No doubt, like Heather, he'd sensed his client — and her daddy's money — drifting away from him. "Good. Good! Ms. McGee, I'll be in touch. No more pets, hmm? Two weeks 'til the party of the year. Ms. Connors's parents' home in the West Hills is simply fabulous! You'll love serving there, simply love it!"

"I'm sure I will," Heather said. She looked about ready to drop. Even her bow tie had lost its jaunty tilt. Isabelle hurried off to gather Marnie's bowl and dog food, grabbing the leash as well. She was relieved that Chloe hadn't pulled the plug on the party, relieved that Marnie was getting out of this apartment where she most assuredly didn't belong, but sad to see her go.

She handed over Marnie's things as Heather, Freddy and Chloe discussed the last of the details. Caressing Marnie's face and rubbing her ears, she said, "Thanks, Rick. For everything." The dog had crumbs on her whiskers while the faint aroma of garlic wafting on her breath led Isabelle to suspect Heather's garlic croutons had become a canine appetizer.

"You didn't leave me much of a choice," he said dryly.

"I know."

"Anyway, I didn't want to see Heather suffer for Marnie's wild streak."

Brushing away the crumbs, Isabelle said, "About this Mr. Charles. Is he your landlord? Will you get in trouble when you bring home a dog?"

"*Now* you're worried about my landlord? Isn't it a bit late for that?"

Isabelle studied his face. She finally said, "I guess it is. But the other day you said your life had changed and you couldn't be responsible for the dog."

"I changed my mind under duress," he said with a smile. "Don't worry about Mr. Charles."

"Just take care of my girl," Isabelle said, kissing Marnie's head. "She's been acting so strange . . ."

Chloe was suddenly at Rick's side. She had obviously decided to make friends with the dog, and she patted Marnie's soft little ears and spoke baby talk to her face. Marnie seemed to enjoy all the attention, which further depressed Isabelle.

Freddy Randy was the last to leave. He was no longer laughing.

"I am so sorry," Isabelle said as the door closed behind the party planner.

Heather looked ready to faint or spit nails. It was hard to tell which.

"I mean it, Heather. My behavior tonight was deplorable. I wouldn't blame you if you sent me packing. I was rude and surly and then the dog —"

"You?" Heather said. "You were a real trooper. It's that stupid Freddy Randy and his stupid client. How dare he suggest a seafood bar after telling me it was to be an hors d'oeuvres party. I cooked my tail off for this sampling. If they think they're getting another one, they're dead wrong!"

Holding her index finger and thumb a bare quarter inch apart from one another, Heather added, "That woman was this close to zeroing in on a menu. This close. She and Freddy damn near ate everything on that table including the flowers. Then Freddy says with that nasty little hee-haw of his, 'Of course, dear, you might want to consider a raw seafood bar. It's very trendy, trés chic.' I'd like to trés chic him! Next thing you know, Chloe 'follow-like-a-sheep' Connors wants a damn raw seafood bar!"

"But Marnie —"

Heather held up the hollowed loaf that was now crimped in the middle and beginning to fold over on itself. "Wasn't that a riot?"

"But you looked dazed. I was worried —"

"I was mad, Isabelle. Furious. Marnie probably saved me from killing your ex-boyfriend's fiancée."

All Isabelle could think was: *Well, shoot. That's too bad.*

Chapter Seven

After Rick saw Chloe home to her seventh floor apartment, he and Marnie rode the elevator down to the lobby. Chloe had asked him in for a drink, but he'd put her off. She'd been really cute with Marnie, calling her sweet names and patting her goodbye, but Rick suspected it was an effort. Chloe wasn't a "dog person," and Rick shuddered to think what havoc the dog could wreak in Chloe's immaculate apartment if ignored for even a moment.

So, he'd declined the invitation and hoped Chloe didn't realize the real reason he didn't want to be alone with her just now was that he wanted to avoid her inevitable questions about Isabelle.

For instance, what had he and Isabelle been whispering to each other when Chloe's back was turned?

Why did Isabelle feel it was okay to foist her dog off on him?

Why had he let her?

Valid questions. Trouble was, there were no satisfactory answers.

Nor did he want to launch into an explanation of what had gone wrong in Isabelle's and his relationship. He'd covered that ground a year before when he and Chloe first met, and he didn't want to revisit it. Not tonight.

At the thought of Isabelle, his lips curved into a reluctant smile. She'd looked so uncomfortable dressed like a butler with that crooked bow tie and her dark hair in a tidy little knot on top of her head. She'd looked as surprised to see him as he'd been to see her.

Much as he hated to admit it — and would to no one other than himself — his farewell visit to Isabelle had created more questions in his mind than it had provided answers. She'd said their kiss was just a kiss and, of course, she was right. So why hadn't he been able to forget it? Why had his pulse doubled when he saw her tonight, why had he resented acting as if he barely knew her, why had Chloe's arrogance, obviously born of insecurity concerning Isabelle's unexpected presence, annoyed him instead of eliciting his sympathy?

What kind of fiancé was he?

Horrible thought: was he still in love with Isabelle?

No. Of course not. What was more likely was that he was using her as an excuse to reconsider his feelings and commitments to Chloe.

And that made him a heel.

So, how did he go about fixing this?

Possibility One: fire Heather and, by default, Isabelle.

He couldn't do that. It wouldn't be fair to Heather.

Possibility Two: confess all this to Chloe.

Yeah, right. Not even he was stupid enough to believe Chloe would want to hear him ramble on about an old girlfriend, unresolved feelings and his own fear of commitment. Get real.

The answer: get a grip.

It was cool for a June evening, and he lowered Marnie's window so she could stick her nose out and sniff the wind. Every once in a awhile she'd look at him over her shoulder. Sometimes, he could swear she was smiling at him. Like now . . .

Try as he might to let the events of the evening fade away, impressions still kept swirling through his mind. Isabelle's surliness, Chloe's tension, Freddy Randy's nervous laughter, Heather's increasing quietness, his own dissatisfaction with the way things were shaping up.

Take the seafood bar. Didn't Chloe know he was allergic to shellfish? He was almost certain she did. There'd been an incident at a restaurant up in Seattle a few months before. Not a serious one, but he was sure she was aware of it.

Nevertheless, once Freddy Randy mentioned a raw seafood bar, her eyes had lit up. What really alarmed him was the distinct impression he'd gotten that she'd warmed to this idea so quickly because she knew her father would approve. Rick was used to his future father-in-law's preferences ruling the office; Gary Connors was the boss, it went with the territory. He just didn't want Chloe putting her father first in her own private married life . . . and his.

Marnie woofed as he pulled into his building's parking lot. As he carried her gear upstairs, she pranced along on the end of her leash as though she owned the place. Unlike Chloe's and Heather's building, his allowed pets under twenty-five pounds, so that wasn't an issue. It was only Mr. Charles he need worry about.

He unlocked his door and switched on the lights, illuminating an apartment he had worked hard to get just right. He'd grown up above a boat works, in a space cluttered with tools and manuals and charts. He'd grown up where "art" consisted of yachting calendars pinned haphazardly to the walls for five or six years at a time; where the furniture was half wood crate, half thrift store; where rugs were woven mats and chandeliers were suspended lightbulbs.

In furnishing his own first real home, he'd chosen Oriental carpets, worn but still luxuriant; a leather sofa and matching chair; decent lamps. He'd collected books he loved and reproductions of wonderful paintings. Nothing first-rate, as he couldn't afford first-rate yet. Someday. For now, he settled on classy copies put together with an eye for detail.

The one exception was a baby grand piano positioned by the two western windows. *That* was a piece of art, lovely both in tone and design, a purchase made from the former tenant who hated the piano because her ex-husband loved it. Rick had happily used his first bonus check to purchase the piano and had spent hours since then refinishing it to get it just right.

At eight o'clock on a summer evening, the waning light cast a lovely golden glow onto the burnished wood. Sheet music that Rick was laboriously trying to learn — a not-so-easy task, seeing as he was only in his second year of piano lessons and, face it, wasn't exactly a natural perched on the stand. The piano represented something meaningful to him and one way or another, he would learn to play it or die trying.

Mr. Charles sat on the piano bench, upright and very regal-looking. Rick sat down beside him and extended a hand.

Marnie suddenly caught sight of Mr. Charles and woofed.

Mr. Charles blinked but didn't show the slightest inclination to move.

"You two better learn to get along," Rick said, running his hand down Mr. Charles's back. Catching Marnie's eye, he added, "There will be no more barking, is that clear?"

Marnie, of course, barked.

Is this why, when Isabelle first asked Rick to take me, he said no?

Because of a cat? Oh, say it ain't so!

Had I successfully conned my way back into Rick's life only to be foiled by a cat? Not just any cat, either. A Siamese with a brown mask, feet and tail and two spooky blue eyes that seemed to follow me wherever I went.

Mr. Charles, my foot.

Of course, being resilient, I immediately took

the upper hand and initiated a conversation with the beast, but just like every cat I have ever met, this one didn't seem to understand a word I said. I suspect cats speak a dialect all their own, one understood only by a few select humans.

Never mind. I would not let a measly cat get in the way of my plans.

My job description was easy: work on Rick from the inside. Get him to thinking about Isabelle, remembering the good times, longing for more. I wasn't sure how much time I had. That other woman alarmed me. For one thing, she had a mean streak, did she not? A little itsy-bitsy one? And she didn't like me. She pretended, but she really didn't, I could tell.

I'd bet you anything she was responsible for Mr. Charles!

I looked old blue eyes over again and made a decision. I would snub him. There wasn't time for distractions. He could go his way and I'd go mine.

As soon as Rick jumped into the shower, I took off on an exploratory trip through every room, sniffing every corner, investigating every open door. Eventually, I became aware I had a shadow; sure enough, old stealth cat was dogging my every step. As per my strategy, I ignored him, even when he followed me into a closet in the spare room.

There was a box in the back corner of that closet that smelled vaguely familiar. I tore at it, growling with determination, paying no attention to the cat's raspy meows or the other stuff in the closet that rattled and shifted around me. I was on a mission!

The cardboard was no match for my teeth, and eventually it peeled away.

Well, well, look what we have here!

Jackpot!

Rick sat up in bed that night working on a pro bono case. He had papers spread from one end of the bed to the other. Mr. Charles was stretched out on the foot of the bed, his head resting on a book of family law, purring. His gaze seemed to be directed to the floor, and Rick looked to see if the cat had deposited a catnip mouse on the rug. He'd unsuspectingly stepped on more than one soggy toy during the night and it always jump-started his heart. The only thing down there, however, was Marnie who had curled into a ball, her eyes tightly shut.

Smiling, he thought to himself that he'd missed the little mutt. She was a sweetheart when you got to know her, upbeat and resilient and feisty. It was good having her here. He should never have refused Isabelle's request in the first place, but she'd called while Chloe was there and he'd been certain that Marnie and Mr. Charles would be enemies on sight.

Apparently he was wrong on that count. It looked as though the two had formed a truce of sorts.

An hour or two later, tired enough to fall asleep now, Rick reached to turn off the light. His hand grazed the framed picture of Chloe he kept by the lamp, and he picked it up to look at it. It took a few more seconds to realize something was wrong with the picture.

Same dark hair, same dark eyes, different woman. It was Isabelle's picture.

The picture evoked a host of memories. A warm summer day, a simple picnic he'd packed seeing as Isabelle's idea of picnic food was crackers and cheese sticks and his was roasted chicken and Greek salad. The river, the grass, the trees. Isabelle caught looking into the water in a contemplative mood, arms wrapped around bent legs, cheek resting against her knees, her hair a glistening black cloud around her shoulders.

Isabelle . . .

He dropped the picture. Where had it come from? Where was the photo of Chloe?

He immediately jumped out of bed and looked around the small table, figuring he must have knocked it to the floor. Maybe he'd stuffed it in the drawer. He searched the top of the dresser and even peeked into his bathroom.

The photo was gone.

Walking back to the bed, he glanced down at the dog. "What do you know about this?" he said.

She didn't crack an eye. But it had to be her; there simply was no other explanation. Where had she found Isabelle's picture and where had she stashed Chloe's?

"Marnie," he said, using his courtroom voice. "What's going on here?"

This time, the little dog opened her eyes and blinked innocently. She yawned, show-casing two rows of white teeth and a pink gullet. Then she rested her head between her front paws and went back to sleep.

"We'll talk about this tomorrow," he warned her as he climbed back between the sheets. He deposited Isabelle's photo in the bedside drawer and slammed it shut.

All the commotion apparently annoyed the cat who sat up, stretched, meowed once and jumped off the bed where he proceeded to settle on the rug beside Marnie. His purr-ing filled the bedroom as he tucked his brown sable nose under his front paw and went back to sleep.

Rick had the distinct feeling something was going on, something he should be able to figure out, something that eluded him. But it was late and he was weary. There were suddenly too many distractions in his orderly life.

Two pets.

Two women.

Too much.

He flicked off the light and closed his eyes. A parade of seafood marched in front of his eyelids. Clams lined up behind lobsters; mussels in front of oysters; caviar rained over all like glistening black hailstones. Just as he was about to drift off, it occurred to him that he would have to invite his father to his engagement party. What would the old man do when he discovered the prospective bride wasn't Isabelle?

This was the stuff of nightmares.

The following days were busy. Isabelle tried to earn her keep by helping Heather cook ahead for a Portland State University Women's luncheon she was catering the coming Saturday. Meanwhile, there was an octogenarian's birthday, a going away party and an order of cream puffs for a local restaurant. To top it off, Heather's pregnancy had entered a new phase; cooking odors now brought about a slightly green sheen to her porcelain complexion. So much for her "cast-iron stomach."

Isabelle was concerned about Heather's hectic schedule, most of it formulated when she had a husband to help her. She couldn't meet all her obligations alone and Isabelle was desperate to get back home. Born and raised in Portland, she hadn't moved to Seaport on a permanent basis until after college when she got her first job, but Seaport was home now and she missed it. Her parents had moved away a few years earlier, and most of her childhood friends were married or living elsewhere.

Face it, Isabelle thought, *Rick's dad is right, life does go on.* Life here in Portland had gone on without her, but that was okay. She just needed to get back to Seaport where her life's path had taken her.

But how could she abandon Heather?

Heather, for her part, refused to talk about hiring help. Since the sampling, she'd grown increasingly moody. Isabelle had taken on a few extra chores, the least agreeable of which was calling Heather's supplier and placing the order for Rick's engagement party. She resisted the urge to cancel the bushels of oh-so-fancy seafood and substitute hot dogs.

Speaking of dogs, she missed hers. Life was certainly more uneventful without Marnie, but it was also lonelier. She tried looking on the bright side, but Marnie and she had been constant companions for almost five years and there was no getting around the fact that having someone you love to care for gave life a definition that went missing when the loved one was absent.

Yes, even when the loved one was a dog.

Three interesting things unrelated to catering happened later in the week. The first one was a chance meeting with Chloe Connors in, of all places, the basement laundry room. Isabelle was running a load of kitchen linens for Heather when Chloe arrived with a basket of her own. This came as a surprise to Isabelle, who had assumed Chloe hired someone to do something as mundane as her laundry.

They met while Isabelle was moving her load to the dryer. Isabelle could tell by the long pause in the other woman's step that she wanted to turn right around and leave, but pride or curiosity or indifference apparently got the best of her, and she set her basket down without glancing in Isabelle's direction.

"Hi," Isabelle said.

Chloe assumed a startled expression as she turned from sorting her whites to stare at Isabelle. "Oh, hi," she said. "Irene, isn't it? Or is it Iola?"

"Neither," Isabelle said calmly. As if you don't remember! "It's Isabelle. We met up at Heather's apartment Sunday night."

"Oh, yes. You're the caterer's little helper."

Isabelle reminded herself that this woman was Heather's client and that Isabelle's cut of Heather's fee to cater Chloe's outrageously expensive engagement party would mean Isabelle could go home sooner. Well, if Heather ever snapped out of her doldrums she could go home.

"You're the one with the dog," Chloe added.

"That's right, Rick's old friend," Isabelle said, enjoying the frown that creased Chloe's forehead. As Isabelle fed the dryer quarters, she surreptitiously peeked at Chloe, wondering what Rick found so attractive about her.

On the surface, she realized, they looked alike. Chloe was better dressed — even to do the laundry the woman dressed haute couture — but their hair and eyes were the same color, their builds more or less the same, even the shape of their faces were similar.

But underneath? She suspected they were

as different as silk from burlap. She suspected Chloe came on kind of adoring and accommodating at first, at least until she felt threatened, and then she got nasty like she had the night of the sampling up in Heather's apartment, like she was acting right now. She hoped Rick understood that this was the kind of woman who changed during marriage. She hoped he knew Chloe was likely to become increasingly self-centered and vindictive as she grew older because it seemed to Isabelle that women like this always did.

She instantly felt guilty for making such an absurd assumption about a woman she didn't even know. Rick was right: meeting your fiancé's former significant other on the eve of your own engagement had to be unsettling. Feeling a wave of remorse for all her bad thoughts and sulky behavior, Isabelle said, "Your engagement ring is drop-dead gorgeous."

And it was. Two red rubies flanked a sparkling diamond.

Chloe glanced at her finger. "Once Rick makes partner, he'll replace this little thing with something more . . . substantial."

Isabelle had to work to keep her mouth from dropping open. Chloe's dismissal of Rick's ring sounded so calculated. Not trusting herself to comment on this without sounding as snappy as she felt, she said instead, "You must be excited about your seafood extravaganza."

Slamming the lid of the washing machine, Chloe Connors planted her fists on her hips and regarded Isabelle with insolent eyes.

"I know what you're doing," she said. "Let's get this straight. I don't give a rat's patootie what you think about anything. If Rick weren't so damn loyal to your friend, I'd change caterers in a heartbeat. So don't try to play nice with me to get to him. It won't work."

Isabelle was speechless — for a second or two, and then anger fueled by embarrassment kicked in. "As long as we're being frank with each other," she said, "why don't you get something straight? I'm being civil to you for my friend's sake. I have no interest in Rick except that he, like Heather, is a friend of mine. Just a friend. You don't need to feel threatened by me."

"As if I could feel threatened by you," Chloe said.

Hands shaking, insides quaking, Isabelle said, "You, Ms. Connors, are a real peach."

Chloe deposited a few quarters in the washer before stomping away. Isabelle left as soon as her dryer stopped, not even noticing until she was back inside Heather's apartment that the linens were still damp.

One fact was inescapable, she thought as she ironed the wrinkles — and the moisture — out of the linens. She was right about the kind of woman Chloe Connors was and probably right about the kind of woman she would become. What was Rick thinking?

The second odd thing happened a day later while walking between her car and the front of Heather's building. She caught sight of a tall man with brown hair walking briskly away. She called out, "John," for she immediately thought of Heather's absent husband, but the man didn't turn or acknowledge her greeting. She asked Heather about it when she got upstairs. Heather, who had just finished baking half a dozen lemon cakes for the deli down the street, looked up in alarm. "John? Are you sure it was him?"

"Not positive," Isabelle had admitted. "There was just something about his build and hair — I got the impression it was him, that's all."

"But what if it was him!" Heather cried, clutching her stomach. "Why wouldn't he have come inside and talked to me?"

"But what if it wasn't him?" Isabelle said, wishing now she'd kept her mouth shut. In the end, because there was no way of knowing for sure if it had been John Isabelle had seen or someone else, and because there was therefore no way to know if he'd been about to come beg her forgiveness or not, Heather had gone into the bedroom to lay down leaving icing the cakes to Isabelle.

The third odd thing happened on Friday when she received a call from Rick asking her if she would come to his apartment that evening. Marnie needed her, he said. He grew evasive when pressed for details. As much as Isabelle wanted to see her dog, she didn't want to run into Chloe again, and so she bluntly asked him if the other woman was invited as well and was assured she wasn't.

"Then I'll come," she said uneasily. "If you're sure."

"Sure about what?" he'd said rather testily. "That I want you to come or that Chloe won't be there?"

"Both."

"For heaven's sake, Isabelle. I just want you to come over for a few minutes and . . . well, reassure your dog. She's been doing . . . odd stuff. Acting strange. I live at Fir Street. Just come." And with that he'd disconnected their call, which irritated the heck out of Isabelle. She had half a mind to tell him to cope with Marnie on his own, but she didn't want to call his office and she didn't want to leave Marnie in the lurch, so instead she spent the next few hours fuming.

By that evening, however, she was more curious than angry. Rick's apartment wasn't situated in quite as upscale a neighborhood as Heather's and Chloe's building. It was smaller, too, and she could reach his second floor apartment by climbing a flight of narrow outdoor stairs. For a second, she was reminded of his dad's place above the boatyard, but as soon as she reached Rick's landing, all similarities vanished.

He'd planted a giant tub of sun-loving zinnias and petunias that formed a mass of primary colors arching and draping with wild abandon. His porch, painted white, accented the blue of his door and a shiny brass knocker tempted her to use it. Also tempting was the worn bench, a tiny little thing set in one corner of the porch, a perfect place to sit in the morning and drink a cup of coffee or retreat in the evening with a book. For some reason, Isabelle was reminded of Mrs. Polk's house back in Seaport, the house Rick had stopped to admire when they'd walked from her place to the beach. Maybe it was the flowers or the blue door.

She heard piano music, and resting her hands on the whitewashed waist-high wall, stood looking over Rick's view of downtown Portland while a sonata floated on the wind. Someone was playing Beethoven on the radio —

A sour note and an abrupt halt to the music suggested this was not a radio but an actual musician. The music started again; Isabelle suddenly realized the music was coming through the wide-open windows at right angles to her perch. In other words, the music was coming from Rick's place.

Another sour note, another false start. She took the opportunity to knock, but as she did so, she heard a female laugh. It was too late to slink away unnoticed.

If Chloe Connors opened that door, she would kill Rick!

Chapter Eight

Rick called out, "Come in, it's not locked."

Marnie woofed a couple of times as though echoing Rick's invitation and Isabelle took a deep breath and pushed open the blue door.

A tiny woman wearing an exquisite aqua, silk tunic stood by the piano. Rick sat at the bench. A Siamese cat perched in one open window while Marnie danced around Isabelle's legs, yipping with excitement.

Isabelle knelt down to soothe and hush her dog. "I'm sorry if I'm interrupting —" she began.

"Oh, no, it's quite all right," the woman said. She looked to be about thirty with glossy auburn hair and huge green eyes. Her skin was as pale as moonlight. "We're running late as usual, but Ricky is getting so good! Did you hear him play? Isn't he spectacular?"

"Yes," Isabelle said, standing. "He's great."

Rick got to his feet, towering over the woman. "Please, you're both embarrassing me. Elena, please meet Isabelle. She's a teacher, too."

Elena held out a slender hand. "You are? You teach music?"

"No, I teach little kids," Isabelle said.

"That's wonderful," Elena said. "Do you love your work?"

"Very much," Isabelle said.

Elena looked into her eyes for a few seconds and smiled. "We're lucky, aren't we? To both have work we love to do?"

"Yes," Isabelle said, thinking that if Rick had to get married, why didn't he chose someone as lovely as his piano teacher instead of Chloe Connors. "Yes, we are."

The woman released Isabelle's hand. "Well, I'd better be on my way. I have another appointment in about ten minutes and it's clear across town. Goodbye, Ricky. Practice hard."

"It was nice meeting you," Isabelle called as Rick saw his piano teacher to the door. Isabelle used the moment they spent saying goodbye to walk to the window where she admired the Siamese cat. He was an elegant-looking animal with a creamy breast, mink colored points and slightly crossed eyes. She longed to run her fingers down his sleek back, but she was allergic to cats. As though he understood, he jumped from the window and curled himself around Marnie's chest, his tail waving in the dog's eyes.

"What do you think of that?"

She turned to find Rick regarding the animals with a bemused expression.

"I'm surprised. Marnie has never seemed to like cats all that much."

"Well, she likes Mr. Charles."

"So, this is your landlord, Mr. Charles."

He smiled down at her. He had a great smile when it came on spontaneously. She wondered how many spontaneous smiles a lawyer was allowed. Five? Six? Was there a moratorium on smiles during the workday? Surely when he was at court he'd have to be cautious . . .

This wouldn't have been a problem if he'd become a boat designer. A boat designer could smile when the mood hit him. Why hadn't Rick wanted to be a boat designer?

"I can't tell what you're thinking," he said, the smile fading.

"I'm thinking your place is charming," she said, moving away a few steps and glad he couldn't read her mind. "I didn't know you played the piano."

"You heard me," he said. "I'm not sure I

can claim to actually play it, but I'm learning."

"Well, it sounded good to me."

He gestured at a folded pink towel sitting on a table. "Be sure to take that when you leave. It's the one I borrowed that day I got wet —"

The day of the infamous kiss. He didn't say it, but there was something in his eyes . . .

For heaven's sake, Isabelle, the man's engaged. Stop doing this!

Doing what? she asked herself, noticing that up close and personal, Rick's facial abrasions were all but healed. He didn't limp anymore, either.

Speculating!

Living up to Chloe Connors's accusations.

He said, "Where was Heather's husband the other night? I was hoping to meet him."

"John? Oh, he's . . . visiting . . . his brother."

"I hope everything's okay for Heather," Rick said, a frown creasing his brow. "She seemed a little upset towards the end. I thought she might be annoyed with the seafood bar thing, but Chloe said caterers were used to catering to their clients needs and I suppose she has a point."

Isabelle did not want to make any further

surly comments about Chloe. She said, "It's probably the pregnancy. I think hormones have got her going a little nuts."

"Pregnancy! Why didn't she say something?"

"Well, it's kind of a secret."

"How much longer will she and John be able to keep something like that a secret?" Rick said.

Searching for any other topic of conversation, Isabelle said, "What's wrong with Marnie? She looks fine to me."

Rick blinked as his mind shifted gears. "Nothing is really wrong with her," he said finally, leaning over and picking up the cat who was rubbing against his leg. The affectionate little animal worked his claws against Rick's muscular chest, shedding a few creamy colored furs onto Rick's black shirt.

"You told me Marnie needed me. Why am I here if she's fine?"

"I didn't say she was 'fine.' Come with me, I'll show you what I mean," he said, depositing the cat once again on the floor. Marnie leading the way, they all stepped into Rick's dining room.

Rick stopped in front of a pale yellow sideboard hand painted with blue cornflowers running along the drawer fronts. White porcelain drawer pulls and a glass-faced hutch gave the piece a casual French-country look. Isabelle immediately loved the piece.

She said, “This is lovely.”

“Do you like it?” he asked, grinning. “I bought it at an antique store. That little one down near the waterfront, do you remember it?”

“The one where you bought my desk,” Isabelle said.

“That’s the one.”

They exchanged a long look until a tawny blur exploded from the floor. With an elegant leap, Mr. Charles jumped on top of the sideboard, barely avoiding tipping over a couple of framed photos displayed there, and then on to the top of the hutch. He sat on his haunches staring down at the humans and at Marnie.

Confused, Isabelle said, “Rick —”

He pointed at the two photos. “Look.”

Isabelle looked. She found a studio shot of Chloe in a gilded gold frame. The slightly larger picture was a snapshot that had been blown up and framed in an inexpensive wood frame that looked vaguely familiar. And then she realized why it looked familiar — it was of her!

She expected Rick to display photographs

of his fiancée, but what was hers doing here? Not sure what she should say, she peered closer. "This was taken the day we picnicked on the Columbia River," she said.

"That's not the point," he said gruffly. "The point is that I'm not sure where Marnie found that photo, just that she keeps finding it no matter where I hide it."

"I don't understand," Isabelle said, thoroughly confused.

"I'm telling you that Marnie found your photo the fist night she was here. She replaced the photo of Chloe on my nightstand with yours and then she hid Chloe's picture."

"Marnie *hid* Chloe's picture? Are you sure, Rick? I mean, I know she's a clever little dog, but to actually 'hide' something —"

"She hid it," he said emphatically, "in the wastebasket."

Suppressing a smile, Isabelle said, "Perhaps it fell —"

"All the way across the room?"

"But —"

"That's not all. She keeps doing it. I go to work, she finds your picture and switches it with Chloe's. I put them back, she does it again. I finally moved everything out of the bedroom thinking that would foil her but it hasn't. And last night I had to work late so Chloe came over to feed Mr. Charles and Marnie. She wasn't too thrilled to find your picture prominently displayed and hers missing."

Isabelle shook her head as she gazed down at Marnie. Was it possible the dog could really do something like this? She glanced at Rick, trying to figure out why he'd make it up.

"Don't look at me that way," Rick said. "I'm not nuts."

"Then throw my picture away. Hang Chloe's picture on the wall where the dog can't touch it. This doesn't seem like rocket science to me."

"Ah," he said, "this isn't all. Come here."

He led her to the kitchen where Isabelle found a folded blanket under the table. "I put this here to discourage her from sleeping on the sofa while I'm at work," he said.

Isabelle thought, *Good luck!*

"I'm not sure if it works or not because she's a crafty little thing and always meets me at the door. But look closely at the blanket."

Isabelle looked; she saw a kind of disgusting mauled pink mouse with a yarn tail and a small stuffed dolphin in among the folds of white blanket.

"She has toys?"

"The mouse belongs to the cat though it spends most of its time in the dog's water bowl." He picked up the dolphin and handed it to Isabelle. "Look closely at this."

Embroidered on the dolphin's fin was a tiny sky blue heart.

"You gave that to me four years ago," Rick said. "We were visiting the aquarium in Newport and you bought it for me. I didn't give it to Marnie; she found it. It turns up in my bed, under my coat . . . here and there. There must be a box of old stuff around here somewhere. I haven't had time to search it out yet, but obviously the dog found it."

Isabelle handed Rick the dolphin. He gave it to Marnie who appeared to be grinning, but that must have been caused by the way holding the dolphin caused her lips to curl up. "It's just a toy," Isabelle said. "It probably smells old or musty or something. Marnie likes things that have peculiar odors. She's a dog."

"Aha," he said, holding up a finger as though making a point. "Let me show you exhibit number three. Come this way."

This time, he came to a halt in front of the answering machine. The Siamese had rejoined them and he jumped up on the table that held the machine, settling into a compact bundle beside a vase of flowers. Isabelle was about to make a crack about the cat jumping on the furniture, before recalling Marnie's habit at her own house of drinking from the leaky faucet.

"In the last five days," Rick said, "I haven't received a single message from Chloe."

Isabelle didn't say the first thing that came to her mind, which was something along the lines of, *Lucky you! I talked to her in the laundry room. You aren't missing a thing.* Instead she said, "I don't think you can blame my dog because your fiancée doesn't call."

"But my fiancée does call," Rick said softly. "Often. She hears my greeting and leaves one of her own but by the time I get home, her message is gone."

Gesturing at the Siamese Isabelle said, "Maybe your cat —"

"No. Mr. Charles has never shown the slightest interest in the phone. This all started the day Marnie came. And mind you, I still get my other messages. It's just Chloe's that are erased."

Though she tried not to, Isabelle smiled.

Rick said, "I don't think any of this is amusing."

Isabelle looked at him and suddenly felt a

wave of sadness envelop her. He really didn't find it funny, and yet of course, it was! How could he not see it? She said, "Not even a little?"

"No."

"Rick, she's only a little, homesick dog. Do you really think she's capable of such machinations? This is all just coincidental. I assure you, there's no evil plan afoot —"

"Chloe doesn't see it that way," he said.

Isabelle's anger, as it was wont to do on occasion, surfaced swiftly. Narrowing her eyes, she said, "So that's what this is about? Chloe is annoyed? What does she think, that I sent Marnie here on some secret mission to foil your engagement? Does that make even a lick of sense to you, because if it does, Rick, you need professional help!"

He stared at her for a second, his dark eyes flashing with annoyance. Maybe she'd pushed him too far, but at that point she didn't really care. Twirling, she took a step away before he caught her arm and twisted her back to face him.

"A canine Mata Hari?" he said.

She smiled, relieved beyond all common sense that the real Rick was still alive and well and living in his own skin. She said, "A regular undercover pup."

Smiling, he let go of her arm. He said,

"I'm sorry, Isabelle. I don't know what came over me."

Isabelle knew what had come over him: Chloe's jealousy.

Again, showing valiant restraint, she bypassed that little observation and said, "I can't take her back to Heather's, Rick. The poor woman is operating on reserve as it is."

"I know you can't. Chloe will just have to live with it for a few more weeks."

"Let's tear your place apart and find this treasure trove of old stuff," Isabelle said with a rush of sympathy. She had a feeling Chloe living with something she didn't like would be harder on Rick than it would be on Chloe. Rick agreed with the plan, suggesting first they have a bite to eat, explaining he'd baked a Cajun chicken the night before. Thinking of Rick's way with spices, Isabelle quickly agreed, and before long, they were eating an impromptu supper on the small porch decked out with zinnias and petunias.

And a dog.

And a cat.

After they ate and cleaned up, they started the search for memorabilia. It took awhile, but eventually, Isabelle found a box in the back of a closet Rick seldom used; once he thought about it, he realized the door had been open for days.

He dragged the torn box out into the room and they sat on the floor, going through the contents. Isabelle looked more relaxed then he'd seen her for years, smiling often, tossing her loose hair, totally unaware of herself. He loved this about her, always had, this way she had of being so oblivious of her own charm, the innocence of her actions and behavior. If she didn't also have a quick temper, she'd be . . . well, she'd be someone else.

At first, Rick was embarrassed that he'd kept so many little things she had given him. A Portland State sweatshirt; a leather-clad daily reminder from years earlier; mugs and knickknacks, books on yacht design and sailing; letters and postcards and dozens of photos.

He had vivid memories of receiving most of it but none of stowing it. Obviously, he'd stuffed everything into a box after their split; he couldn't imagine why. The box must have moved with him two or three times before being warehoused in this closet.

She held up a mug covered with stylized sailboats, the price sticker still stuck to its side. "You didn't use this?" she asked. "I remember thinking it was so pretty. It made me think of your dad's beautiful boats."

He stared at it a second before remembering the day she gave it to him. Should he be honest with her or make something up? Deciding on honesty, he said, "You gave that to me the day before I told you I was going to law school. You were very upset, don't you remember?"

She looked embarrassed as she bit her lip. "I remember."

"So, I didn't feel much like drinking coffee out of that cup."

"And then you left," she said, setting the cup aside.

"No," he said firmly. "Then you left."

She regarded him with her dark eyes, so like Chloe's and yet so infinitely different. "You left," she insisted.

Marnie, who, with the cat, had taken up position on the bedside rug a few feet away, yipped. He glanced at the dog who seemed to peer back at him through anxious eyes.

But Rick wasn't about to give in on this point. "The second I told you about my new plan, you started leaving me, Isabelle. You were so disappointed in my choice of career, *in me,* in fact, that you drifted away. All I did was say the actual words we both knew were inevitable."

She stared at him for a second before swallowing hard. "We had plans," she said at last and he saw her eyes suddenly glistening. "I was going to teach, you were going to work with your dad —"

"But that was never really *my* dream."

"But you said —"

"Isabelle," he said softly, "I was young. There was a lot of pressure. My dad had his ideas —"

"And I had mine. That's what you're saying."

"I'm saying that plans and dreams change. It's love that should withstand the shifts that happen to everyone, love that should be enough. But for you, *for us,* it wasn't."

"That's not true," she said, rising quickly, spilling the small remembrances of their years together to the floor. She stared down at him. "Sure, I was upset, of course I was upset. I hadn't realized how many pre-law classes you were taking, you hadn't seen fit to tell me. I didn't know you'd applied for law school. You'd been making plans in secret and then you expected me to just roll over and say, 'Whatever you want, honey.' "

He was standing now, too. "Damn right that's what I expected you to say."

"But that's not fair," she said, nearly stamping her foot with the injustice of it all.

"Maybe not," he said, "but it's what people do for the people they love."

"You are living in a fairyland," Isabelle said. "Chloe Connors has got you bamboozled."

"Leave Chloe out of this —"

"Gladly."

"Chloe Connors has done nothing but be supportive."

"Chloe Connors knows how to get what she wants. She'll agree to anything if it furthers her goals, surely you know this about her. I bet there isn't an honest bone in her well-clad body!"

Now Rick felt like stamping his foot. Had Isabelle always been this hardheaded? The cat had fled at the first sign of raised voices, but Marnie stood between them, fretfully looking from one to the other as though she understood they were in the midst of a heated argument and was trying to arbitrate a settlement.

It's hopeless, he wanted to tell her. *There can be no settlement between us. . . .*

Isabelle said, "Pack these things back into the box and put it in my trunk. Then Marnie won't be able to trot them out for your fiancée and you won't be on the receiving end of her wrath. I'm leaving."

And with that, she turned tail and made

good her promise. He heard the slam of his front door a moment later, and began re-boxing his old things, Marnie watching his every move, whining occasionally. Mr. Charles surveyed the proceedings from the top of the bed frame where he'd taken refuge once the fur began to fly.

A moment later, he rounded up Isabelle's old picture and the stuffed dolphin, dumped them resolutely into the box with everything else, grabbed the pink towel from the table and carried the whole thing out to Isabelle's car. She was sitting inside, the motor running, the trunk lid popped open. He put the box in the trunk, closed the lid and hit the car with his open hand. She was gone without a backward glance.

Marnie, who had followed him outside, woofed.

Is it just me, or have things gone from bad to worse?

Needless to say, a fight was not in my plans. I'd wanted them to get hot and bothered when they walked down memory lane, but not in the knock-down, drag-out way.

Had I been wrong to think these two people belonged together? Was my dream of a united family just that: a dream?

No. Of course not. Silly me. And then there's

Charlie. True, his quick paw was useful snagging things I couldn't ferret out of small spaces and even I had to admit he never failed to divert attention at the right moment, but he is a cat and a dog has certain standards. He slept on my blanket. He watched me eat. He followed me everywhere I went and even gifted me with his moth-eaten catnip mouse, which he persisted in depositing in my water bowl. Blech.

I put him on the back burner of my mind as I tried to focus on my main dilemma, namely, Isabelle and Rick.

I would have been willing to bet a month's worth of chew bones that Isabelle cried all the way back to Heather's apartment and that made me feel terrible. She was my primary responsibility in life and I knew she needed me, but there she was, driving off alone. Rick just stomped around his apartment, yelled at me and the cat a little, slammed a few cupboard doors and buried himself in paperwork.

That's one thing old blue eyes and I had in common. Neither one of us took offense at Rick's surliness. I thought I understood why he was acting that way, and I honestly don't think the cat gave a hoot.

Maybe it was time to admit defeat and get Isabelle and myself back to Seaport. But how did I do that? Now that Rick had accepted me into his home and Isabelle had taken all her belongings away, I had no leverage, I was stuck, wasn't I?

The cat sauntered by just then, and it occurred to me that if I gave him some major grief, Rick might insist Isabelle take me back. Snapping, biting, growling — I could come up with something. Once back with Isabelle, all I had to do was jump on Heather's counters a couple of times, and presto, Isabelle and I would be on our way home.

The plan lacked verve. I lacked enthusiasm.

Remember how I said a wire fox terrier never gets discouraged?

I admit it; I was discouraged. And as I nosed old stealth cat off to a corner of my blanket and curled into a tight little ball for a bit of shut-eye, I had to confess I didn't have the slightest idea what to do about it.

Chapter Nine

Chloe's parents lived on an estate in the West Hills of Portland. The house itself was built on a hillside with a terraced yard that seemed to flow into the border of trees and perennials at the bottom of the property. A twisting road gave the illusion of country, but the view from the many patios was pure city. Isabelle guessed half a dozen gardeners made it their life's work to keep everything trimmed, mowed, deadheaded, fertilized and watered.

The house was huge and white, multicolumned and multistoried. Giant shade trees dipped gracefully overhead. She imagined the entrance to the house was equally graceful, but she didn't get to see it as the hired help were asked to use the back door.

The extra servers Heather had hired met them in the kitchen, and the next few hours were spent in final food preparation. Isabelle tried to do everything she could to reduce the stress on Heather who was obviously not sleeping or eating well. Heather had commented that the raw seafood bar had turned out to be a blessing in disguise as there wasn't much cooking to do, hence there were none of the odors that sent her stomach into spasms.

Frankly, Isabelle wasn't sure how much longer Heather could hold on to her business by herself; Isabelle knew she was just barely making things easier for Heather, as she lacked the knowledge and intuition of a chef. Therefore, she'd stepped up her campaign to get Heather to call John and get him back where he belonged.

The seafood bar was to be positioned in the solarium. The sky, trees and flowers in the backyard, visible through the glass walls and ceiling, made the space seem to go on forever. Isabelle watched as an ice sculpture, in the pose of a playful dolphin, was positioned in the middle of a large round table. She heard Heather giving directions for both the raw and cooked seafood to be set up in circles around the base. It turned out there wasn't room for the salmon puffs, Chloe's last-minute addition to the party fare, so Isabelle volunteered to offer partygoers the fragile creations from atop a silver platter.

Freddy Randy supervised decorations that seemed, in the midst of so much natural beauty, to be gilding the lily. His spurts of nervous laughter punctuated the draping of every horizontal surface with white linen spread over the top of pink cloth, the placing of baskets of white lilies and tiny pink rosebuds, the lighting of a zillion little white candles in clear glass containers and the hanging of huge gold-foiled doughnut shapes from every available rafter. They looked like little UFOs to Isabelle but she was told rather sternly that they represented wedding rings.

Whatever.

From then on, she kept her opinions to herself. Her only desire was to get through this party, shake some sense into Heather, retrieve her dog and get the hell back to Seaport. She did not want another confrontation with Chloe, nor did she want to see or speak with Rick. She had no idea if Rick's father had been invited to the party or if he'd come. She didn't care. She intended to do her part quietly, efficiently, and from the background.

Chloe's father turned out to be a very well-preserved man in his early fifties with prematurely gray hair that was still thick and wiry. He had dark eyes like his daughter.

His current wife was a good thirty years younger, a platinum blonde who seemed nice enough, but the belle of the ball, and rightly so, was Chloe.

She wore a pink-and-white off-the-shoulder dress that looked so simple you knew it had to cost an arm and a leg. She looked very good in the dress, which made Isabelle feel even frumpier in her black slacks, white shirt and black bow tie. She fought the urge to tear off the bow tie, untuck the shirt, and let her hair tumble around her shoulders. She felt invisible.

Oh, yeah, she reminded herself, *that's exactly what you wanted.* And yet she resented blending into the background.

She was a mess.

It didn't help that Rick showed up looking dashing. It didn't help that she saw him kiss Chloe's cheek and toast her with champagne.

Isabelle busied herself passing the puffs.

While she was doing this, she picked up snippets of conversation. Apparently, her lowly service status rendered her deaf as well as invisible; people spoke freely in front of her.

One matronly woman said to another, "Chloe's stepmother is younger than she is!

It's shameful," as she snagged two salmon puffs.

The other woman nodded, took a sip of champagne and said, "She's his third wife, each one younger than the one before. Number four will still be in diapers!"

"And Chloe's own mother wasn't even invited to this shindig!"

"She wouldn't have come," said the champagne sipper. "Lana is currently touring Europe with her fourth husband. But isn't Chloe's young man handsome! I hear he has a brilliant future."

Actually, Isabelle heard many comments about Rick, mostly from women, and mostly about his dashing good looks. As per Chloe's wishes, Rick's scrapes and bruises had healed beautifully; he'd look great in all the candid pictures the roving photographer was taking.

Two men pushing sixty were so deep in conversation, that Isabelle decided to wait until they came up for air to offer them salmon puffs. She gathered they were talking about a third man. She heard the assertion, "No one else would work with Chesterfield on that Holgate business. Everyone's afraid of the fallout should he fail."

Holgate. Why did that ring a bell?

The other man said something about the

case dragging on to the end of time as he turned to find Isabelle at his elbow.

"Salmon puff?" she said.

The first man took one of the delicate hors d'oeuvres and waved it absently at the other. "Connors did good when he hired Manning, that's all I'm saying."

"He could have gotten my nephew for half the money, that's all I'm saying," the other man said.

Isabelle was interested in the comeback, but just then a hoard of elderly ladies gathered round and nothing could be heard over their excited chatter. They wiped the platter clean.

Eventually, despite her earlier vow to mind her own business, she began to wonder why she hadn't seen Rick's father. His absence seemed ominous to her, portending continuing tension between father and son at the very least and perhaps something more. She decided to see if she could corner Rick — just Rick — and ask him about it.

Okay, so that wasn't the real reason she wanted to speak to Rick. She regretted her part in their last fight. She liked Rick, she always had and always would; even if they couldn't be lovers, did they have to be enemies?

To provide camouflage during her search,

she returned to the kitchen to refill her platter. She found Heather sitting on a stool outside the back door, looking a little green around the gills. "Are you okay?" Isabelle asked.

Heather fanned her face. "Not really. The smells are beginning to get to me. Those salmon puffs pushed me right over the top. Oh, Isabelle, what am I going to do?"

"Stay out in the fresh air for now. I'll get you a glass of cold water. When we get back to your place tonight, you're going to call John and invite him over. You two need to talk."

"But —"

"No buts. I'll hold your hand if you want, but Heather, you need him to come home and it's time to admit it. Stay here, I'll be right back with your water."

After delivering the water, Isabelle refilled her tray and started making the rounds again, looking for Rick. The dolphin ice sculpture in the solarium had gone from frosty to glossy, the inevitable downward spiral of ice to water. She made her way outside to a lovely enclosed patio where she finally found Rick talking with another man.

Not wanting to intrude, she skirted them both until she saw who the other man was and then she almost dropped her platter.

"John!"

She hadn't realized she'd spoken out loud until his gaze swiveled to meet hers. "Isabelle!"

Rick looked at her with a scowl. How disheartening, she thought fleetingly until she recalled that she'd been the one to walk away from him the last time they met. She had to admit that she more or less deserved the look he now cast her way and she tried a conciliatory smile. It was so much easier to be mad at him when she wasn't actually facing him.

The smile got her nowhere.

She turned it, instead, on John. "What are you doing here?"

"I wangled myself an invitation from the bride-to-be's father. My firm used to handle his accounting before he outgrew us. He introduced me to Rick. We were just comparing notes."

Notes about what? Or whom?

Isabelle said, "I don't understand. Why did you wangle yourself an invitation?"

John blinked a couple of times. "Because I wanted to come," he said at last. "I *had* to come."

"Then you know Heather is here. You know she's doing this party."

"Of course I know she's here," John said.

"I was there when she booked it, though back then it was supposed to be an hors d'oeuvres party. Listen, the other day I saw you going into my building."

"I thought I saw you, too. Why didn't you answer me when I called your name?"

"I didn't want to talk to you," John said. "I'd come to see Heather, to apologize, but I just couldn't think of a way to back down." He shook his head and added, "Stupid pride," under his breath.

Isabelle cast Rick a nervous glance. Had she told him that John didn't know about Heather's pregnancy? She racked her brain — while trying to keep up with the current conversation — but couldn't remember what she'd said to Rick and what she hadn't. Finally, realizing that John was waiting for some kind of response to a question or observation she hadn't heard, she shrugged and hoped that would take care of it.

"Don't get me wrong, I'm grateful to you for supporting her," he said, "but I have to tell you that I intend to move home as soon as possible. If she'll let me."

"I thought you were looking for your 'space,' " Isabelle said softly.

A red flush stole up John's neck. "She told you about that, huh?"

"She mentioned it."

"She was just acting so weird, Isabelle. Laughing one moment, crying the next . . . I didn't know what to make of it. Then she wanted to come on a dull old business trip she'd told me earlier she didn't want to go on, meaning I'd have to make last-minute changes not only to my own plans but those of two coworkers and I got to feeling that I needed a couple of days to myself to think things through. She went ballistic."

Isabelle hurried to speak before Rick could. "She's sitting outside the kitchen, John. Go find her."

"That's why I'm here. I thought a nice, neutral spot would be better a spot to . . . discuss . . . things than in our living room." With this, he looked at Rick as though apologizing for using Rick's engagement party as a neutral spot to talk to his wife who was supposed to be working.

Rick said, "Don't pregnant women often have mood swings?"

Isabelle winced.

John's jaw dropped.

Rick, not understanding what he'd just done, said, "I don't know firsthand, of course, but I've heard that hormones go haywire."

John looked deep into Isabelle's eyes.

"Heather's pregnant?"

She could see no way out of this, so she nodded.

"Where is she?" he demanded. "In the kitchen? I have to find her." And with that he walked off in a trance.

"Why do I feel like I just let the cat out of the bag?" Rick asked.

Isabelle said, "You didn't know she hadn't told him yet. I'm glad you clued him in. Maybe now the two of them will have a real talk. It's way past the time that they do."

"A 'real' talk," Rick said, casting her a distrustful frown. "I'm not so sure 'real' talks accomplish much, Isabelle."

She decided not to respond though she knew perfectly well what he was alluding to: their real talk of a week or so before when they'd admitted they'd both felt abandoned by the other. The talk had accomplished nothing, just as Rick said, except to open old wounds. She said, "I don't see your father. Didn't he come?"

"He couldn't. He's in the hospital."

"What happened? Is he okay? He isn't okay or he wouldn't be in the hospital!"

"Calm down," he said, taking her elbow in one hand and the serving platter in the other. The platter he set aside on a table; Isabelle he guided to a cement bench flanked by two ceramic pots filled to the bursting points with ferns, moneywort and lilac-colored impatiens.

"I've been in Seaport the last two days," Rick said. "Dad felt light-headed Thursday afternoon and one of the yard crew called an ambulance. Once they got my old man to the hospital, they started running some tests and decided a brief stay and an adjustment to his medications were in order. I saw him yesterday evening. He was doing pretty well. He's being released today. He's worried because he's a little behind schedule. The doctor says he can go back to work on the sailboat in a couple of days, so he's about as content as he ever gets."

Isabelle took a deep breath. "Did you have a chance to tell him about your engagement? What did he say?"

"Well, he actually smiled and patted my back and told me he was sorry to miss the party."

"I'm glad you told him," Isabelle whispered, feeling such an exaggerated sense of loss that it took her a moment to remember to breathe again.

"I took Marnie with me," Rick said. "She loves riding in the car, doesn't she? Had her nose out the window the whole way there and back. I locked her in Dad's apartment while I was at the hospital. Mr. Charles stayed home, of course."

"Where did you get that name?" Isabelle asked.

He smiled warmly and Isabelle felt a sigh swell in her breast. Rick was such an attractive guy, inside and out. He deserved better than Chloe. Truth was, Isabelle suspected, he deserved better than her, too. He said, "Believe it or not, the cat showed up on my doorstep in the pouring rain about six months ago, skinny as a rail and howling like a banshee. I ran an ad in the newspaper, knocked on the neighbors' doors, put signs up on telephone poles — nothing worked. It took him about two days to elevate his status from the cat I fed to the cat who slept on the end of my bed. The vet thinks he's a year or so old and judging from his comfort level with Marnie, I'd say he might have come from a home with dogs, but more than that, I just don't know."

"And his name —"

"I thought he deserved a dignified name," Rick said. "I was going to start calling him Charlie after a while, but Chloe took to the mister part and it just stuck."

"He's sure beautiful."

"He must have been someone's pet," Rick said. "I can't believe how well he's getting along with Marnie. I actually think those two will miss each other when it comes time for you to go home, Isabelle."

"I imagine that day will come sooner rather than later. But I'm glad we've had a chance to talk today."

"I am, too."

"And I'm glad your dad finally got to a doctor."

"Good thing, too. The doctor threatened him with fire and brimstone if he doesn't stop sneaking smokes. He's just so stubborn."

"He's not the only stubborn one," Isabelle said softly. "Rick, I need to apologize for being so catty about Chloe. I shouldn't have attacked her."

"Believe it or not, I understand. I need to apologize, too."

She tried to think what he might be apologizing for, but came up blank. "What did you do?"

"You were right the other day. I did make plans to attend law school in private. I knew you'd be upset, I knew my father would throw a gasket, so I took the easy way out and just did my own thing. I didn't give either one of you a chance."

Isabelle put her hand over his. "All this is in the past," she said. "You have a good future ahead of you and so do I. As your father always says, life goes on. Listen, I've been hearing nice things at this party about you."

His eyes brightened as though he was relieved to let go of the past. "Like what?"

"Ooh, all the little old ladies think you're quite a hunk and the men call you brilliant. There was something about a guy named Chesterfield and something about Holgate which sounds familiar to me, though I can't think why —"

He sat up straighter as his dark eyebrows knit together. "Who did you hear that from?"

Isabelle glanced around the patio but she didn't see the two men she'd overheard talking. "Two older guys," she said at last. "One was tall and aristocratic-looking and the other one had a reddish goatee."

"Chloe's uncles," he said right as Chloe made an entrance onto the patio. Her gaze was pleasant as she glanced around at her guests; pleasant, that is, until she caught sight of Isabelle and Rick sitting together.

While Isabelle immediately looked away, she was aware that Chloe was making a beeline in their direction and she felt her heartbeat accelerate. Come what may, she was going to be polite to Chloe Connors. It was the woman's engagement party, for heaven's sake, and Isabelle had no desire to ruin it for her — or Heather. Taking a deep breath, she was surprised when Rick stood abruptly and without saying goodbye, intercepted his fiancée and steered her back inside the house.

Feeling thoroughly dismissed, Isabelle waited a few moments before following them inside. She made her way to the kitchen where she found Heather crying in John's arms, both of them oblivious of the bustling activity around them. From the desperate way they gripped each other, Isabelle realized husband and wife were back together and that the sooner she left town, the better.

Would she have enough money to replace the carpet Marnie had destroyed? She wasn't sure, but Heather must owe her at least enough to make a few payments. The summer was only about half over. Maybe she could get a temporary job at the Coffee Hut down near the beach to help with the rest.

But money wasn't the real issue, and she knew it. She needed to get out of town because she still had feelings for Rick and he was taken. It wasn't fair to him or Chloe or herself. Her presence here wasn't good for anyone.

She needed to go home and forget Rick.

Again. . . .

Rick's kitchen window looked out over an alley. He usually kept the blinds slanted, but on Sunday afternoon, the day after his engagement party, he had them open in the hopes something outside would intrigue him enough to keep his thoughts from racing around in circles.

It didn't work; he couldn't concentrate.

In the other room, Chloe's voice rose and fell as she rehashed the party with one of her friends. It struck him that she was a woman with many friends. In fact, at times, the sheer number of cohorts it took Chloe to do just about anything, from buying shoes to eating lunch, amazed him.

But — weren't women supposed to befuddle men? Wasn't that expected? Didn't his future father-in-law allude to the mystery of women the same way some people refer to the possibility of life on other planets?

She'd been on the phone for a long time now and it was beginning to irritate him. He needed to talk to her. Closing the blind, he went back into the room to coax her away from the phone, but she waved him off.

Mr. Charles was on top of the hutch, shoulders hunched, tail switching. Marnie sat at the bottom of the hutch, gazing up at the cat. Rick had noticed that Marnie didn't bother the cat unless Chloe was around, which seemed perverse and totally mysterious. But these terms more or less described Marnie, at least lately.

He clipped the leash on the dog and let himself outside, taking Marnie with him. He sat on the old bench he'd stuck in the corner of the porch and the dog jumped up beside him, her tags jangling together like bells, the little lilac heart-shaped tag catching the sunlight and sparkling like a jewel.

The sun felt good on his face. He closed his eyes and Chloe's voice coming through the window began to fade. Even the traffic assumed a gentler sound, kind of like ocean waves but more constant. If there had been a little wind, he might have been able to convince himself he was in Seaport. The perfume of the petunias and droning of a bee lulled him . . .

"Hi!" someone called, and he knew who it was even with his eyes shut. He opened them to find Isabelle staring down at him. Marnie had jumped into her arms, and woman and dog were both smiling.

"I tried to call," she said.

"Chloe's on the phone, but I have Call Waiting. I wonder why she didn't she answer."

"Maybe she hates Call Waiting."

"Maybe." He stared at Isabelle. She looked lovely in a dainty rose-colored blouse that complemented her skin and highlighted the natural color of her lips. Wisps of hair framed her oval face, and he fought the sudden urge to brush them away. He said, "I guess she's in the middle of an important call."

Isabelle shrugged. "I wanted to warn you that I was coming to pick up Marnie," she said. "I'm on my way home."

"Then Heather and John made up?"

"Big-time. They need their privacy, and I need to get back to the ocean air."

"That's . . . great," he said.

The front door opened and Chloe peered out. One look at Isabelle and she said, "You again? You never give up, do you?" then turned right around and went back inside.

"I'll get Marnie's things for you," Rick said. "Come on in."

"I'll just wait out here," Isabelle said, glancing at Chloe's retreating form. Leaving the front door ajar, Rick gathered Marnie's belongings: her dishes; the new bag of food he'd just bought; the box of treats he'd spoiled her with. He dumped everything into a paper grocery bag.

Chloe sat on the couch, leafing through a magazine in jerky little movements. He knew as soon as Isabelle left, Chloe would have a few choice words for him, which suited his needs fine. He had a few choice words for her.

He paused at the front door. Isabelle perched on the bench, Marnie beside her, Mr. Charles up on the railing, gazing slightly cross-eyed at the dog. "Here," he said, handing over the bag of dog stuff.

Isabelle got to her feet. They stared at one another for a moment before she reached out and touched his hand with tentative fingers that she quickly withdrew.

"Thanks," she said.

He realized suddenly that he had to make her understand that there could never be anything between them. The pull they had to one another was undeniable — but it was also hopeless. He didn't want to hurt or embarrass her, though. He said, "You're welcome."

"I'll check on your dad when I get back and call you if there's something you should know."

"Don't worry about it," he said with as casual an attitude as he could muster. "I talked with him this morning. He's home from the hospital and doing fine. I wouldn't be surprised if he's back to work tomorrow morning. You go ahead and enjoy the rest of your summer and don't concern yourself with my father . . . or me, okay?"

The flicker of disappointment he saw in Isabelle's eyes told him that she'd extrapolated the meaning of his suggestion: *Back off.*

Sometimes a man had to be cruel to be kind. Isabelle had to understand that this was their last goodbye.

"Take care," he added.

With a nod, she was off, Marnie trotting alongside her, both of them disappearing down the stairs and out of his life . . . forever.

He glanced over at the cat who stared down the stairs after them. . . .

Chapter Ten

As long as I live, I will never understand humans. Why do they complicate their lives the way they do? Why do they fight so hard not to be happy?

Consider the dog. Left to his or her own devices, romance is fleeting but lots of fun. No strings. No angst.

Given their need to make something enjoyable into something difficult, couldn't humans just be honest with themselves? Judging from these two, not so much. . . .

So now Isabelle and I were on our way home. She was sniffling, wiping her eyes occasionally, and mumbling under her breath. I was glad to get away from the cat, but sorry Rick wasn't driving as he always put the window down for me and Isabelle seldom did. Plus, Rick sometimes stopped at the fast food place on the edge of Portland and fed me French fries as he drove. If Isabelle broke up the two-hour drive to the coast at all, she did it by stopping at a park alongside the river and taking me for a walk.

Don't get me wrong, I like walks as well as the next dog, but she never let me off my leash to swim in the river and she never let me sniff around the picnic tables or trash cans, so overall, Rick's French fries won paws down.

There was a point in here somewhere. Ah, human foibles.

Oddly, my depression began to lift the closer we got to Seaport. Through the power of my psychic thought, had I not convinced Isabelle to take us home? I might lack a definitive plan, but I still had my telepathic powers of persuasion. All I had to do was stay on my toes and take advantage of any opportunities Isabelle provided.

You see, I'd watched hers and Rick's faces when they said goodbye. I no longer doubted that they truly wanted to make a decent home for me, hopefully somewhere far away from Ignatz, the poodle, who, I had just recalled, would be waiting for me once I got back to the duplex. Groan. He made even stealth-cat look good by comparison.

I'm digressing again. Leave it at this: my happiness — and theirs — depended on me 'cause they sure weren't going to do anything about it.

It was time to hone my skills. As Isabelle sniffled and sighed, I chanted in my head: Rick, Rick, Rick though I have to admit I was really thinking, French fries, French fries, French fries . . .

No one's perfect.

Isabelle stopped her car in front of Carl Manning's boatyard. It was late Sunday afternoon, and she'd spent two hours and a hundred miles trying to decide if she should obey Rick's oblique command to forget about his father's welfare or follow her own instincts and check up on the old guy.

She was still undecided.

Rick wanted her to stay out of his life. That was obvious and understandable. The possibility that he might have discussed this situation with Chloe to come up with some kind of plan of action made Isabelle's skin crawl.

Wait. Would Chloe have suggested something as subtle as what Rick did or would her proposition have been more along the lines of, "Point a bazooka at her head and pull the trigger?"

Isabelle soon grew weary of her own indecisiveness. Carl Manning was her friend; he had been for years. If Isabelle wanted to visit him, she'd visit him. Rick could lump it. Chloe could stuff her bazooka where the sun didn't shine.

She snapped on Marnie's leash. The large street-side gates to the boatyard were chained and locked, but there was a smaller door cut into the wire fence. It, too, was locked, but someone working inside saw Isabelle jiggling the handle and decided she didn't look dangerous. She thanked the man for opening the door for her.

As it was late Sunday afternoon, the only people present seemed to be boat owners working on their high-and-dry vessels. The large building where Carl Manning built his commissioned sailboats and accessed his living quarters seemed to be locked up tighter than a drum and for a moment, Isabelle worried that the old man had had a relapse and was at the hospital again.

Marnie was sniffing and scratching the small door off to the side. Isabelle recalled this was a second, seldom-used entrance that led upstairs to Carl's living quarters. She knocked on it and tried the handle. It opened with a creak and a groan, and she called out a greeting.

She heard a faint hello hollered back and the command to come on up.

She and Marnie found Rick's father sitting in a recliner. The television was on, but with the volume turned so low Isabelle decided they'd caught him drowsing in his chair.

"I'm sorry to bother you," she said, leaning over to kiss his cheek. He was wearing his usual outfit: denim pants, ticking shirt, red suspenders.

He said, "You could never bother me. I'm real glad to see you. Get us a couple of cold drinks from the fridge and sit down for a while."

Isabelle got the drinks, fighting the urge to wash the sink full of dirty dishes in Carl's small kitchen. However, years before, she'd tried straightening and cleaning for him and had been told in no uncertain terms to leave things as she found them. She took the cans of soda back into the living room and handed him one, looking around for a spot to sit, finally clearing away a stack of magazines from the seat of a matching recliner. Marnie had tucked herself into the chair beside Carl.

"Do you want me to fix you something to eat?" she asked him.

He drank half the can in one swallow. "No thanks." He gestured at an empty pizza box on the floor beside his chair and added, "I already ate. Sorry there's none left to offer you."

"No problem," Isabelle said, her stomach perversely growling at the mention of food. "Well, you've had an exciting few days."

Absently patting Marnie's wiry head, Carl sighed. "Damn hospitals. Hard to get a moment's peace in the blasted things."

"I know. Rick told me you had trouble."

He snorted. "Bunch of overreaction, that's all. First Gus got all excited when I got a little light-headed, then them doctors got to going and once they start testing, you're lucky to make it out alive."

She made sympathetic noises. "I'm just glad you're okay."

"Listen, honey," he said, leaning toward her and wearing a concerned look that seemed kind of foreign to him. "I'm real sorry I missed the party. Real sorry. That son of mine finally does something right and I miss it. Did you have fun?"

He must be under the impression that she'd been at Rick's engagement party as a guest! Seeing no reason to go into details right that moment she said, "Sure. Of course. It's great to see Rick so . . . happy."

"You think he looks happy?" Carl Manning said. "See, I don't. He looks preoccupied to me. Man about to be married should be whistling, should be smiling, but he just looks worried."

"Do you think so?"

"Yep. And I know it can't be because of who he's marrying, so it must be that damn job of his, wearing him down. He won't talk about it, but I suspect the dullness gets to him."

This topic of conversation was pointless as far as Isabelle was concerned. Where once she would have agreed with Rick's father's assessment, now she wasn't so sure. Spending a little time with Rick recently had made Isabelle reconsider some of the conclusions she'd reached years before. She'd begun to suspect that Rick was following his dream by being a lawyer. She was beginning to see that she and his father had put a lot of pressure on him to follow *their* dreams. Law wasn't dull and routine, not to Rick.

She smiled and didn't say anything.

He said, "Well, that's for him to figure out, isn't it?"

"Yes," Isabelle said emphatically.

"Now, tell me all about your party."

"*My* party?"

"Yours and Rick's engagement party! Did your folks come down from Seattle? Did you have a band? Dancing? Beer, wine, what?" Chuckling, he added, "Did my son get down on one knee and propose proper-like or did he send you a summons or something? Come on, honey, I want details!"

Isabelle stared at him with her mouth open.

"Isabelle?" he said.

What should she do? He was under the impression that Rick was engaged to be married to . . . her!

Had Rick not mentioned his intended's name? Had he left out that one teensy-weensy detail?

Carl patted her hand. "Cat got your tongue? That's okay, I'm a little tired anyway. How about you come back in a day or so and don't forget to bring your little mutt."

For the first time, Isabelle realized that Marnie had left Carl's side. She got to her feet and called for Marnie, who didn't respond. Looking around the cluttered apartment, she could catch no glimpse of Marnie's tri-colored back sniffing for pizza crusts or what have you.

"Marnie!" she called again.

This time, the dog trotted out of the back of Carl's apartment, back where the bedroom was. Knowing Carl, he'd eaten toast in bed. Knowing Marnie, she'd quickly cleaned up the crumbs. Isabelle ducked her head into the bedroom just to make sure everything was in order; Marnie had been acting awfully odd lately. Other than the usual clutter — stacks of old newspapers beside the bed, clothes strewn here and there, shoes abandoned in the middle of the floor — everything looked okay.

"I'll come back soon," Isabelle said, gathering the soda cans and returning them to the kitchen. Carl had drained his; she put her unopened can back in the fridge.

"Bring pictures if you or your folks thought to take some," Carl called from his chair.

Pictures!

She needed to call Rick. He needed to come clear up this misunderstanding!

But how could she call a man who had gone out of his way to make sure she understood she was to stay out of his life?

She'd figure it out tomorrow or the next day. Right now, she was suddenly ravenous. Surely there was a frozen something or other at home she could nuke for dinner.

But she didn't want to go home, and the thought of microwave food after dining on Heather's delectable creations left her cold. She didn't want to stop and see friends, she didn't want to talk or think or do anything else that would even remotely remind her of

Portland or Rick or marriage or fun or the future. . . .

So, what *could* she do?

Pulling the car over to the curb, she found the perfect solution: walk on the beach. Maybe after that, she would find a fast-food restaurant and satisfy a sudden craving for French fries. . . .

Rick went into the office early Monday morning in order to work before the office came alive and his first client arrived.

He'd done his articling with a man named Bert Chesterfield, whose practice occupied the third floor of a dilapidated old building near the waterfront. Bert described himself as an aging hippie and took pride in the fact that half his clients made him all his money, while the other half made his job worth the while.

During Rick's articling, Mrs. Henrietta Holgate, the elderly widow of a lumber baron from way back when, expired, leaving a huge tract of coastal land to a non-profit organization. The only caveat was that just enough timber be harvested to finance a camp for disabled kids. As Chesterfield explained it, the woman felt guilty about her husband making all that money cutting down trees and this was her form of atonement.

The only problem was that this part of her legacy bypassed all six of her children, ages fifty-eight to seventy-three, who knew that the standing timber on the land that wouldn't be harvested was worth millions. Agreeing on something for the first time in fifty years, they'd hired a hotshot lawyer and claimed undue influence on the part of the organization's founder, Marilee Jot, who had befriended Mrs. Holgate before her death. Bert Chesterfield, meanwhile, represented Marilee Jot, pro bono. The preliminary hearing was ongoing; Rick was helping Chesterfield collate data and do background checks, routine behind-the-scenes kind of stuff.

It had jolted him when Isabelle mentioned overhearing Chloe's two uncles talking about the Holgate case at his engagement party. He made it a practice not to talk about this case, mainly because it wasn't his to talk about. He'd obviously mentioned it to Chloe; it wasn't a secret, after all, but he didn't like being the subject of gossip, personal or professional.

Once the firm's office started coming to life and arriving coworkers' voices could be heard out in the halls, his concentration was shot and details of his personal life began bombarding his consciousness.

It had been an eventful weekend.

Chloe's father peeked in his door. "I need to talk to you," he said.

"I'll be right there," Rick said, signing off his computer.

It promised to be an eventful week, as well.

During the few weeks she'd been away, homesickness and a tendency to look on the bright side of things had caused Isabelle to remember Mrs. Pughill as a nice elderly woman with a cute little poodle and a heart of gold.

Monday morning took care of that.

Isabelle was awakened by a thundering knock on the door that started Marnie howling. "Hush," she scolded as she shuffled to the front door while throwing a sweater on over her nightgown. Blinking at the morning light, she beheld her landlady.

Gone were the brassy curls. The puggish woman had apparently decided to dye her hair red. Something had happened during the procedure, however, as the poor woman was now almost bald with just a few crimson hairs dancing in the northwesterly breeze.

Isabelle couldn't stop staring at her landlady's head. Maybe if she'd been more awake she could have dissembled better, but half-asleep and disgruntled to boot, those few waving red hairs were quite eye-catching.

A shrill bark near the ground finally got through to Isabelle who looked down to find Ignatz hovering near Mrs. Pughill's sock-clad ankles. His watery eyes looked as belligerent as ever.

With wakefulness came the remembrance of the giant hole in the carpet behind her, and Isabelle attempted to hold the door tight against her hip. The throw rug was still on top of it, or at least she thought it was, but the truth was she hadn't thought to check as she made her way to the door and who knew what Marnie had done during the night?

"You're back," Mrs. Pughill said. Ignatz snarled as Marnie stuck her nose out the door and sniffed. "And *that* dog," Mrs. Pughill added. "You still have *that* dog."

"Yes, I do. Is there something I can do for you, Mrs. Pughill?"

"My sister had babies," she announced. "I have to go help."

Isabelle had met Mrs. Pughill's sister, Leticia Harrison, when she stayed for a week over the holidays. The woman had to be at least sixty! "Babies?" Isabelle repeated, unable to believe her ears.

"Babies!" Mrs. Pughill said again, louder this time as though Isabelle might have returned from Portland with a hearing problem. "I have to go help."

"Uh, what kind of babies?" Isabelle asked.

"Puppies," Mrs. Pughill said as though Isabelle was daft. "Three of those little weenie dogs. Dachshunds. Leticia is in a dither. She's a spooky little thing."

"Leticia?"

"No, the bitch."

"Your sister is a —"

"The mama weenie dog is a bitch," Mrs. Pughill said, clearly exasperated with Isabelle's denseness. "I'm leaving right now for Spokane, Washington. I'll be gone for three days. I want you to pick up my paper and keep an eye on the place. Read the horoscopes every day. I'm a Scorpio. If something looks bad, I expect you to call and warn me."

"They have horoscopes in Spokane," Isabelle pointed out, dreading the thought of becoming Mrs. Pughill's personal astrologer.

"Their paper doesn't carry Madame Hortense," Mrs. Pughill insisted. "And open your curtains, let some sunshine in your half of the duplex. All that dark is bad for the carpet. I almost went in and opened up the place while you were gone but I know how you are about your privacy. Still, I can't abide mildew on that brand new rug."

Isabelle, giving up, said, "I'll be happy to look after the place."

"And read my horoscopes."

"Mrs. Pughill —"

"It's the least you can do, seeing as how I give you such a good deal on the rent. Promise?"

Three days. How bad could it be for three days? Besides, another thought had just entered Isabelle's head. She said, "I promise. Drive safely. Have a good trip, Ignatz."

When Ignatz snarled, Marnie growled and tried to barge her way past Isabelle's legs. Isabelle managed to close the door before Marnie could start a fight.

"Bad dog!" she scolded, leaning against the door. The scatter rug was bunched up against the wall, the hole in the carpet in clear view, looming larger than the Grand Canyon.

Marnie, undaunted as usual, trotted into the kitchen.

The first thing Isabelle did after Mrs. Pughill drove away was call the carpet store. Mrs. Pughill leaving like this was a gift from heaven; if Isabelle moved fast enough, the landlady would never know about the hole.

The carpet store, however, suggested they install the new rug a week from Thursday.

"Tomorrow," Isabelle said.

"No way," she was told. "One of the carpet layers is out with a cold."

"I'll pay a bonus if he works with the sniffles. Or hire someone to take his place. This is an emergency."

In the end, the store demanded a ten percent bonus for next day delivery. Isabelle told them to come. She'd worry about the money later.

They promised to send someone out to measure the space just to confirm the measurements she'd given them before she left town. Isabelle locked Marnie in the backyard while the man, wielding a fifty-foot tape measure, came up with the same numbers she'd come up with using a yard-stick.

When she opened the front door to let the man out, who should be on the front step but Marnie! Isabelle had forgotten the little dog had figured out how to jump the fence to get out of the backyard.

Marnie pranced inside with all the self-assurance her breed was famous for. The man with the tape said, "Do you have some place to put this mutt when we're here tomorrow?"

"I'll lock her in the bedroom."

"Good," the man said.

As Isabelle closed the door behind him, she stared at Marnie, who had arranged herself into a sphinx shape next to the hole she'd created weeks before. The dog appeared to be deep in thought.

No doubt plotting a new way to cause trouble.

It occurred to Isabelle that if she couldn't put Marnie in the backyard, where *could* she put her? Locked in the bedroom might keep her off the street, but what about the carpet in there? Would it be safe from her sharp claws and teeth? And what about the fact that Marnie had escaped Heather's bedroom? Her own bedroom had the same kind of handle. The kitchen had durable linoleum, but it didn't have a door. That left the bathroom.

And the bathroom had the same lever style handle as the bedroom! Why didn't doors have knobs anymore? It was a conspiracy!

She had to get out of the house. Taking Marnie with her, she drove in mindless circles until a growling stomach reminded her dinner was overdue. Stopping at the grocery store, she dashed inside to restock her freezer and buy fresh fruit and vegetables.

She returned to a blizzard but not that kind that blew snow day and night. After depositing the groceries in her trunk, Isabelle had opened the driver's door to find that Marnie had shredded a full box of tissue.

Tears filled Isabelle's eyes as she surveyed the mess. She felt pressure build in her chest. She felt alone and . . . trapped. She wanted to call Rick, she wanted to hear his voice, she wanted him to rescue her!

What a dreamer she was. What a fool! Rescue her from what? A box of shredded tissue? Her own disappointments? Her inability to let go of the past and move forward?

Rick wasn't hers to lean on. Rick belonged to Chloe.

This thought caused the tears to roll down her cheeks. For the first time, she admitted that leaving Rick in Portland had been dreadful. Knowing he was going to marry Chloe Connors was dreadful. Understanding that she would seldom, if ever, see him again was dreadful.

She'd sucked up her broken heart before, but now in the face of this minor disaster, she fell apart.

Marnie whined sympathetically.

"Too little, too late," she mumbled as she dug in the tissue box for something with which to mop her face. Of course, the box was empty. In the end, Isabelle opened a new roll of paper towels she'd just bought at the store and used a sheet to dry her tears. Then she did the best she could to de-tissue her car.

"Tomorrow, I'm buying you a dog kennel," she informed Marnie who had stretched out on the back seat as though exhausted from her handiwork. She was covered with tissue bits and in her current ungroomed state resembled a small sheep. She didn't look the least bit upset.

The trouble with living in a very small town was that things closed up at night. The pet store and hardware shut their doors promptly at 6:00 p.m. "And I'm buying a chain so I can chain you to the fence out back," she said as she drove. Though she knew this was an idle threat, it felt good to bluster.

"You may think you're the destructive alter ego of Houdini himself," she added as she brushed away stray bits of fluff stirred by the car's circulating interior fan, "but you're just a little dog."

Marnie roused herself to issue a sharp, "Woof!"

It sounded a lot like a challenge.

Chapter Eleven

"Day One: Not everyone will be as pleased with your plans as you are. Back off if someone you know puts up a fuss. Two stars."

Isabelle folded the paper. Looking at Marnie, she said, "Maybe there's something to this stuff after all. Maybe Mrs. Pughill's sister isn't thrilled that Mrs. Pughill and Ignatz have arrived to see her through her puppy crisis. What do you think, Marnie? Does this sound portentous to you? And what do those stars mean? Should I call our landlady?"

Marnie didn't even bother to bark.

Laying the newspaper aside, Isabelle found a rope. She used it to tie Marnie to the fence as the carpet layers tore up the old carpet.

"That your dog?" one of the men asked a couple of hours later. The job was taking longer than anyone had expected because of a snafu — namely, the men had forgotten to bring the carpet padding with them and one had to return to the warehouse to get it.

Isabelle had been aware of the noise outside, of course. She'd been ignoring it.

"Don't mind her," Isabelle said.

"You better come look, lady," the worker said. He was standing in front of the kitchen door, looking out the little window. Isabelle looked out the larger dining room window.

Marnie had dug under the fence and escaped . . . all the way into Mrs. Pughill's yard where she'd proceeded to circle the landlady's umbrella-style clothesline pole to the point that she was now, literally, at the end of her rope.

"Looks like she's about to choke to death," the worker said, slipping a throat lozenge into his mouth. He'd been coughing and sneezing — obviously, this was the guy with the cold.

Isabelle bit back a snappy retort and went out the front door, around the building and through the gate into Mrs. Pughill's yard.

"You are trying my patience," she said.

Marnie panted.

Untying the rope from her collar and attaching the leash she'd brought with her, she took the dog back through the gate. The carpet van pulled into the driveway the same moment an old red pickup screeched to a halt in front of her duplex. She caught a glimpse of a speckled roll of padding through the van's window right as she heard her name bellowed. At that same moment, Marnie tugged hard and Isabelle felt the leash slip through her fingers.

She gave up going after the dog when she saw Rick's dad walking across the lawn, stiff-legged and angry, a rolled-up newspaper in his hand, the door to his truck left wide open in his haste.

The door was on the traffic side, though there wasn't much traffic this time of day. She should warn him to close it. A car could come by . . . As he got closer and she saw the look in his eyes, she found she couldn't utter a word.

"What's the meaning of this!" he demanded.

Isabelle wasn't sure what to say because she wasn't sure what he was talking about. "I —"

"Is this some kind of joke?" He thrust the newspaper at her and it fell open to the society page of a month before. Rick's smiling face gazed serenely. Chloe looked arrogant.

"Oh," she said.

"Is this a joke? If it is, I don't think it's funny!"

The carpet men, hefting the rolled padding on their burly shoulders paused as if to listen. Isabelle frowned at them. They took the hint and carried the matting inside.

"It's not a joke," Isabelle said softly. "This is the woman Rick is going to marry."

To her dismay, tears glistened in the old man's eyes. He took a red bandana out of his rear pocket and wiped at his face. Isabelle felt warm tears slide down her own cheeks.

"Why would he tell me it was you he was marrying?"

Isabelle suspected Rick had told his father the truth but that his father had chosen to hear what he wanted to hear. She said, "I'm sorry you had to find out this way. Call Rick, he'll explain."

"But you and him . . ." His voice trailed off.

Are not to be, Isabelle thought with a sadness that seemed to have no end. She said, "Rick is marrying Chloe Connors, just like it says in the paper. You'll . . . like her. She's very nice."

And pigs can fly!

"Why didn't you tell me?" he said, his voice cracking.

"I didn't know how," Isabelle said gently. "I knew Rick would clear it up as soon as he visited again."

Carl Manning grabbed her and folded her in a hug. His sympathy was the last thing in the world Isabelle wanted. She needed to be resilient and tough.

He seemed to sense this and within a few minutes, took leave without a backward glance. Isabelle felt a terrible sense of loss that only got worse as she realized she didn't have the slightest idea where Marnie was.

The sneezing worker interrupted her frantic search. "Hey, lady, you'll never believe me, but I think we brought the wrong carpet!"

He was wrong, Isabelle reflected as she began the search for her dog. She had no trouble believing him.

I'd never ridden in a truck before, especially buried under a discarded jacket on the passenger side floor. I found half a pack of peanuts down there, too! Huzzah!

I waited until we got back to Rick's dad's place before announcing myself. Chuckling, he called Isabelle and told her he had a stowaway. As I predicted, she made no protest when Rick's dad insisted he keep me while she finished with the carpet people. All my efforts to prove how incorrigible I was had paid off!

"Well, it looks like you and me are going to spend the day together," he said as he hung up the phone and patted my head. The man packed quite a pat, too. It felt as if my brain had rattled around inside my skull for a second or so. Anyway, as he picked up a chisel and began working on his boat, I curled up on a pile of rags and closed my eyes. Under the guise of sleep, I sent out psychic waves, urging Rick's dad to take some kind of action.

By now you will have guessed that I dug through the newspapers in his bedroom that first day Isabelle and I got back in town and stopped for a visit. While she and the old man had talked about Rick's engagement party, I found the right article and left it where he would eventually notice it. This was no easy task, mind you. Most humans take that opposable thumb thing for granted!

Why did I do this? Obviously because I sensed Rick's dad could prove to be a valuable ally if he only knew what was going on. As for the truck ride? That was just me making use of an opportunity when it presented itself.

So, I concentrated real hard and eventually

I heard a scream and a string of expletives that would have made a pit bull blush. There was blood everywhere!

Sometimes my powers amaze even me!

Isabelle surveyed her new carpet with a critical eye, but even knowing where the old bedroom rug stopped and the living room carpet began, she couldn't see the seam. The workers may have had a rocky start but they'd eventually gotten their act together and completed the job by late afternoon.

And it looked good. Mrs. Pughill would never be the wiser.

The problem of what to do with Marnie during the day was more difficult to figure out than replacing some carpet. Isabelle hated the thought of locking the dog in a kennel for eight hours at a stretch, but she could hardly afford to replace the carpet every time the dog got a wild hair, either.

All worry about Marnie's destructive behavior vanished the moment Isabelle pulled into the boatyard parking lot and found Rick's blue-gray convertible parked in front of his dad's building.

She *really* didn't want to see Rick, especially in front of Carl. What *was* he doing here, anyway? Had his dad summoned him? More to the point, how could she pick up

Marnie and avoid seeing Rick?

As she sat in the car and considered her options (none), the side door opened and Rick exited the building. *At least I'll be able to face him without an audience,* she thought as she got out of her car.

Rick had come downstairs to retrieve his overnight bag and put the top up on his car. He stopped dead in his tracks when he caught sight of Isabelle approaching. She wore blue jeans and a tight-fitting Seaport T-shirt. As always, she looked young and unaffected, though the way her breasts bounced when she walked was anything but innocent. And those hips . . .

Lustful thoughts for a Tuesday afternoon. Thoughts he hadn't allowed himself to think for a long, long time.

"I didn't expect to find you here," she said, coming to a halt right in front of him.

Clearing his throat, he said, "Marnie called me."

Isabelle screwed up her face. "What?"

"Marnie called me."

"What are you talking about?"

"Dad —"

She interrupted him with a hand on his arm. Her eyes wide with alarm, she said, "Oh, Rick! You don't know! Your father discovered that you're really marrying Chloe Connors and he got very upset. Apparently, he misunderstood it when you talked to him in the hospital. He thought you and I . . . that it's me —"

"I know," Rick said, covering her hand with his. "I've already explained. Everything is fine."

She looked relieved then confused. "Did you say Marnie called you?"

"It's like this," he began as her hand slipped away. He shoved both of his into his pockets. "Dad gouged himself with a very sharp chisel today. He's never done anything like that before. Gus took him to the emergency room where they stitched up his left hand and sent him home on painkillers. Meanwhile, Gus locked Marnie upstairs, she somehow knocked the phone off the hook and somehow it ended up speed-dialing my cell. I have caller ID and when Dad didn't answer, I got concerned and drove over here. Dad and Gus were just getting back from the emergency room."

"Good heavens," Isabelle said, sighing. "What will that dog do next?"

"Well, it's pretty advantageous that she did call," Rick said.

"How do you figure?"

"Dad would never have told me he was

hurt. He only has three weeks left to finish this boat or he forfeits a good bonus. Thankfully, what's left to do is mostly finishing work which I used to be pretty good at, so I'm taking some vacation time and staying here to help him."

Isabelle said, "What about Chloe . . . ?"

He shook his head.

"What does that mean?"

"I'm not getting married," he said succinctly, hoping she would leave it alone. He should have known better.

"Why?" she said.

"I'll tell you what I told Dad. It's none of your business."

"But you two were okay at your engagement party! What happened? What about your job? Will her father fire you?"

"You are the most curious woman on the face of the earth," he said. "My job is fine. I think Chloe's father is relieved."

"But poor Chloe —"

"Please don't try to tell me you give a hoot about 'poor Chloe.' "

"Maybe not a whole 'hoot,' " Isabelle admitted with a smile.

"Chloe is fine. She was more in love with the idea of a wedding then she ever was with me. And the rest is, I repeat, none of your business."

She stared at him, biting her lip, drawing who knew what conclusions before finally saying, "Well, as it so happens, I'm currently free as a bird. How can I help your dad?"

"You can make me something to eat," came the gruff reply from the open door behind them. Isabelle and Rick both turned. Rick's dad had come downstairs, bandaged hand tucked against his chest, Marnie at his feet. The dog trotted over to Isabelle, and she leaned down to tousle her ears.

"Dad," Rick said patiently, noticing how haggard his old man looked in the bright afternoon light. "As long as you're taking those pain pills, you shouldn't be going up and down these stairs without help."

"I'm about to starve to death," his dad complained.

"How about hot dogs?" Isabelle said, straightening up.

"You know how to cook hot dogs?" Rick teased.

"As a matter of fact I do, Mr. Smart-Aleck. But in this case, I was thinking I'd drive over to Billy's Seashore Dogs and buy a half-dozen chicken-apple sausages with the works."

"Sounds good to me," Rick's dad said.

"No sauerkraut for me," Rick said.

■ ■ ■ ■

Day Two: You may have trouble keeping the lid on something important. Emotional matters may escalate if you let jealousy cloud your vision. Two stars.

"Another Madame Hortense observation Mrs. Pughill can live without, wouldn't you say, Marnie?"

Again Marnie ignored her.

Isabelle was preoccupied herself. She didn't know what to make of Rick's announcement. There was obviously a story behind his decision to not marry Chloe, though the fact that he wouldn't discuss it might mean that she was the one who had broken the engagement. Either way, had Isabelle contributed to their problems?

If so, she figured she'd probably saved Rick an unhappy few years and a messy divorce down the road. A man like Rick couldn't love a woman like Chloe Connors. Why? Well, because a man like Rick was supposed to love a woman just like . . . Isabelle Winters.

Yes, it was true, she admitted to herself. She was still in love with Rick Manning. Not that she'd ever admit it to anyone. She loved him and just being near him and knowing he wasn't going to go home and marry Chloe made her heart sing.

The following days were jam-packed. There was Mrs. Pughill's paper to retrieve every morning, her horoscope to read, the decision to call her with dire warnings or not. (*Not* always won.) Mrs. Pughill had left a message on Isabelle's answering machine on the third day, telling Isabelle her stay had been extended another week, maybe two, maybe even three. Isabelle was to recycle the papers but keep the horoscopes.

Why? What good were old horoscopes? Did she keep a scrapbook of them? Did she compare each day's selection with a diary account? It was a mystery to Isabelle.

Day Three: You may do more for others than for yourself today. Rewards will come if you are patient. Four stars.

Day Four: Postpone important decisions. Don't let anyone coax you into doing something you aren't fully prepared to do. Two stars.

Day Five: People may not agree with you. Weigh the pros and cons and do what you feel is best. Two stars.

Was it just Isabelle, or was each horoscope so open to translation that they applied to everyone's life? She dutifully cut them out and stacked them near the front door.

By the end of week one, she had a new problem in the form of a kitten who showed up on her doorstep. There was no ignoring the kitten's plaintive mewing. Isabelle took her door to door until she found a neighbor who informed her the kitten's former owner had skipped town, rent unpaid, and no thanks, they didn't want a kitten. Isabelle then contacted the local shelter that promised to find a home for every animal they took under their wing, and was told the place was overcrowded. She was advised to take it to a vet for a checkup, then provide it a foster home until a permanent home could be found.

Sneezing, eyes watering, Isabelle made a safe place for the kitten to sleep in a towel-lined box and placed it in the kitchen. She fed her morning and night, played with her when she could, and asked everyone she met if they wanted a cat.

All this happened against a backdrop that formed the best time of Isabelle's life. She and Rick worked together within the small confines of the sailboat's interior, sanding and varnishing bulkheads and cabinetry, attaching last-minute fixtures such as gimballed kerosene lanterns and galley hardware.

Carl Manning's list of things to be done

that required a person with two hands seemed to grow rather than diminish, and though Isabelle ended each day so tired she could barely talk, she also finished each day wishing it would go on forever.

The Rick she'd fallen in love with was back! The man who worked wonders with his hands. The man who played straight man to his father's and Isabelle's banter. The man who teased her. The man who jogged on the beach with Marnie. The man who occasionally looked at her in such a way that her heart melted, soared and did flip-flops all at once.

He's on the rebound, she admonished herself. *You don't know what happened with Chloe. If she's the one who called it off, might she not decide to call it back on? Would Rick jump if she said jump? Perhaps he's aching for a reconciliation, perhaps he can't wait to get back to Chloe.*

Be careful. . . .

But how can a person be careful with love?

She needed to know what happened with Chloe, yet every time she attempted to find out, Rick deflected her questions. It wasn't until two weeks had passed that he finally sighed deeply and said, "You're not going to give this up until I spill my guts, are you?"

She'd asked him if he planned on calling Chloe when he got back to Portland.

"You're like a dog with a bone," he added.

She shrugged.

The three of them had fallen into the habit of eating a light dinner together after which Carl watched TV, Marnie policed the floor for fallen crumbs, Isabelle was allowed to wash the dishes, seeing as Carl's hand was still bandaged, and Rick closed up the shop. Then Isabelle would drive home with Marnie, feed the kitten and dangle a bit of string for her to play with, then fall into an exhausted sleep until the morning when she would drive back to the boatyard and start the cycle all over again.

On that night, Rick followed Isabelle to her car, but before she could unlock the door, tugged on her arm. "Are you up to a walk on the beach?" he asked her.

Marnie spun around in circles and they both laughed. "Sure," Isabelle said.

It was a moonlit night, and the tide was out. As Marnie ran on out ahead, Isabelle and Rick fell into step beside each other. She had never been so aware of another person as she was of him. Her stomach felt tied in a knot.

This walk brought back so many memories. The high moon, the shadowed beach,

Rick right beside her, tired and yet totally alive and awake and anxious. It was like a giant clock had rolled back time, as though the last few years were footprints on the sand that high tide had suddenly washed away.

They walked for what seemed like miles, Marnie running out in front, full of energy after so many days of relative inactivity. They walked until a creek cut through the beach and it was a matter of getting wet up to their knees or turning around.

They turned, Marnie catching up with them, shaking the sandy water out of her fur and trotting alongside. It was time to have Marnie clipped to wire fox terrier standards: short on the back, longer on the legs, face shaved except for eyebrows and whiskers. She always looked so cute when she was groomed properly, though her current look — wooly and sheeplike — was also adorable.

This was crazy! An empty beach, all the quiet two adults could ever want, and she was thinking about dog grooming? *Come on, Rick, it's obvious you want to say something. Say it!*

She decided to break the ice. "Who's taking care of Mr. Charles while you're away?"

He said, "The neighbors. He's actually

staying at their place so he won't get too lonely."

"Have I told you about my foster kitten? I'm red-eyed all the time now, but what else can I do? The shelter is looking for a home for her."

"It's funny how cats find you, isn't it?" he said.

"Hmm," she said. This conversation had moved them nowhere. She'd hoped he might suggest she start taking allergy shots so she could visit his place more often. Maybe she should be more blunt. "Working all day on a boat and taking a walk on the beach at night sure brings back a lot of memories, doesn't it?" she asked, glancing up at his moonlit profile and feeling her heart pound.

He stopped and so she did. His face, cast in shadows, looked thoughtful. He said, "You used to get cold down here. You used to shiver, even though you wore layers of clothes."

And she used to snuggle in his arms where she was always welcome. She didn't say that. Instead she said, "I guess I've acclimated."

"Yeah. And I play the piano and have a cat."

"And I'm a teacher."

"And I'm a lawyer."

"Your point?"

"My point is that we've both changed. We've moved on."

"Now you sound like your father," Isabelle said, her stomach slowly contracting into a lump. This was not remotely romantic, nor was it related to Chloe and his breakup.

More than that, it sounded like a warning. Was it possible she'd misinterpreted his stolen glances and lingering touches? Had she imagined there was something magical once again growing between them?

Looking down at her feet, she struggled not to feel as scared as she suddenly felt. She said, "That's true, of course."

He resumed walking, then paused and looked back at her. After a moment or so, she caught up with him. This time, it took a quarter of a mile to loosen his tongue. They were opposite the old sawmill, its abandoned structures ghostly in the moon-drenched night. "A man shouldn't get involved with a woman when he still cares for another woman," he said.

For Isabelle, the last quarter-mile had transformed disappointment into anger. The tears were gone. At least she now knew where he stood with regards to Chloe. He still "cared" for her. Isabelle felt like the biggest loser in the world. She said, "Words to live by."

"Yeah," he said. "But I didn't live by them."

Something was wrong with the syntax of that statement, but before Isabelle could figure it out, he'd taken her by the shoulders and turned her to face him. He said, "I've never gotten over you, Isabelle. I've tried, Lord knows I've tried, and I almost convinced myself I had. But the truth is that I never did and I don't think I ever will."

Isabelle was stunned into silence.

He touched her hair. "Isabelle?"

"I don't know what to say," she whispered, afraid he might evaporate if she . . . if she what? Believed him?

His fingers trailed down her face, around her ear. "I never got over you," he said softly. "I tried, but you were always on my mind. I don't know what it is about you, Isabelle. At times it seems like we're meant to be —"

She threw her arms around his neck and he lifted her off her feet. There was a hot eagerness to his kisses that blazed a trail through her body.

"Oh, Rick," she cried, cupping his face and kissing his eyelids, cheeks and chin.

"I've missed you. I've never stopped missing you."

He held her close. "I told Chloe that I didn't love her," he whispered. "I had to. I couldn't go through with it. I was attracted to her for all the wrong reasons. I've made a mess of things."

"Thank goodness, you called it off," she said. "Thank heavens."

"I wasn't sure how you felt."

"Now you know," she said with a laugh. The world suddenly felt very bright. She was amazed stars weren't streaking across the black sky. "I thought you were sending me away for good," she said, taking his hand and kissing his palm. Looking up into his dark, fathomless eyes, she added, "That last day at your place when you told me to forget you —"

"I *was* sending you away," he said, caressing her cheek with fingers so warm and a touch so gentle that it took her breath away. "I knew after our talk at my engagement party that I couldn't marry Chloe. I realized then that what I felt for you wasn't just the ache of past regrets. But I was convinced I needed to let you go. I thought I needed to start fresh."

"But —"

"But then Marnie called and I saw you

again and I realized I couldn't let you go." He kissed her again, longer this time, his mouth hot, his arms strong. "Isabelle, we need to talk," he said when they came up for air. "The last few days with my father have been —"

"Haven't they been wonderful?" she gushed. "That's what life will be like now. You and me, working together, the ocean, Marnie . . . all of it."

"Yes. You and me, yes, it's been wonderful. Of course, it's also been a time out of time. Not exactly reality —"

"A time out of time," she gushed, loving the sound of that. "Oh, Rick, I'm so happy!"

He stared at her a second before whispering, "I'm glad you're happy, Isabelle."

"I love you," she said without hesitation. The words seemed to come from the very depth of her soul. They'd been lurking down there for years, waiting to get out, and saying them felt wonderful. "I love you," she said again.

He met this declaration with a tender kiss that sent shivers from head to foot.

It wasn't until much later, as she lay alone in her bed, that she realized he hadn't said the words back.

Chapter Twelve

I admit I wandered off once Rick and Isabelle started kissing. There'd been an interesting lump of seaweed that begged investigation — anyway, distracted as I was, I could have sworn I heard the word *love* drift my way. I'd thought my job was done. I was ready to pack my dog bones and move to Portland.

So why was Isabelle tossing and turning?

And, by the way, what's with this kitten?

Day Fifteen: You'll be in a sentimental mood today. You will find your own unique niche. Five stars.

Isabelle cut out the horoscope and put it with the rest before feeding the animals and almost flying to the boatyard. She'd spent a sleepless night, reliving every word she and Rick spoke to one another the night before. The nuances, the interruptions, every pause now came back to haunt her. She felt as though she'd missed something important but she didn't have the slightest idea what it might be.

It would all be okay once she saw him.

She drove into the boatyard in time to see Rick unlock his car door. He was carrying a duffel bag and wearing sunglasses and a button-down collar instead of the paint stained jeans and sweatshirt of the past two weeks. Fighting back a stab of irrational panic, she parked her car and ambled toward him.

"Hey," she said, wrapping an arm around his torso. "What's up?"

He gave her a distracted kiss that set off alarms in Isabelle's heart. The sunglasses didn't help as she couldn't see his eyes, couldn't gauge his expression. "I have to go to Portland," he said, opening the door and tossing his duffel bag inside. "I'll try to be back in a couple of days, but sometimes things go wrong. I'll call."

In disbelief, she stared at him. He was leaving? Now?

He said, "It's an important case. There are extenuating circumstances. I became involved in a —"

"I can't believe this," she interrupted. A sound like gushing water filled her head. "You're leaving your dad in the lurch. And for what? To jump when some lousy law firm says jump! You have no scruples!"

He reached out to her. "Calm down, Isabelle."

"I don't want to calm down! What about your father? How can you leave him when there are only nine days to go before he has to deliver his boat?"

"If at all possible, I'll be back in two days," Rick said. "One way or another, I'll get the job done. This is important, Isabelle."

"More important than your father?"

He pulled off his sunglasses and stared at her. All she could think of was the night before when moonlit tenderness had filled his eyes. Now he seemed to be in the throes of another emotion: supreme aggravation.

She was suddenly aware of Marnie pressing against her leg, of the fog bank burning off toward the ocean, of rush-hour traffic picking up on the street outside the boatyard.

And she was suddenly so afraid she could hardly breathe. Why was he acting so distant and cold? What had happened? Was this a side of Rick that went with the courtroom? Had the left side of his brain kicked in and stolen away the Rick she loved? All she was certain of was that they were at a crossroads of some kind; she was not sure what to do or say to break this stalemate.

"If you believe I care more about my career than I do about my father, it's clear you think very little of me," he said at last.

"Rick —"

"No, listen to me. We're going down the same path here as before. It must be nice for you to see the world in such clear-cut black and white. I see lots of shades of gray."

"I think all you see is gray," she whispered.

"I'll be back in two days," he said.

Rising to the bait, she said, "I may not be here."

His eyes looked troubled now. He said, "I hope you are. Things were said last night that need clarification."

Isabelle knew immediately that he was referring to her declaration of love. "You have a nice time in Portland," she said coolly.

He put on his sunglasses and climbed into his car. Isabelle stared at the ground and didn't look up until she heard the roar of his engine as he accelerated out into the traffic and was gone.

"I knew he'd go back to Portland first chance he got!" Carl Manning said from the open doorway. For a large man, he'd sure perfected going up and down those stairs like a phantom.

How much had he heard?

Isabelle didn't respond. Her stomach felt queasy.

"One minute he's talking about modifying the chart table over the quarter berth, and the next he's answering the phone and talking to some bozo named Chesterfield about a Mrs. Holgate. He has to go to some trial, he says. He'll come back, he promises. All I know is my hand is all cut up and I can't work and there are only nine days left before that dentist in California wants his boat ready to launch."

The name Holgate once again rang a bell; Isabelle's head throbbed with the futile effort of remembering why. "I'm here," she said at last. "I can paint, let's get to work."

And work she did, like a demon, staying too busy to agonize over who said what to whom. She quit at seven-thirty when Marnie's whining got too loud to ignore. On the way home, she stopped by the library, aware she smelled like varnish but not really caring. She spent a few minutes using the microfiche machine, then went back out to the car and drove home.

Tomorrow, she would work just as hard. And the next day and the next. After that, Rick would be back and she would be gone.

Rick carried his briefcase through the

labyrinth of halls that constituted Portland General Hospital. He'd been here several times already and had no trouble finding his way to the right room where he knocked briefly on the door before heading inside.

A beautiful woman with long, graying blond hair stood by the single occupied bed, though the empty bed near the window indicated someone else was away having tests or had recently been released.

The woman turned and smiled when she saw Rick, and he kissed her cheek. "Laura, how's the patient?" he whispered because Bert Chesterfield, right leg suspended in an apparatus, left arm splintered and jutting out at an odd angle, seemed to be asleep.

Laura led him toward the window. "Finally sleeping. Who knew he was so resistant to painkillers? How'd it go today?"

Rick set the case down on the empty bed. "The judge threw it out," he said with a big smile. "He said the lawyers had stonewalled long enough, it was time to start honoring Mrs. Holgate's last wishes. I talked to the opposing lawyers afterward. As Bert probably told you, he'd suggested to Ms. Jot that she offer to involve Mrs. Holgate's heirs in planning the camp, hoping that doing something for other people might ease the pain of losing all that money."

Bert's wife said, "That's my man, always thinking the rest of the world is eager to do the right thing if they're given half a chance. What did their lawyers say?"

"They said they were going to take the case to the State Supreme Court."

They both smiled. Rick said, "I don't think they have a leg to stand on."

"Neither does Bert. But if we'd had to petition for a continuance, it would have meant additional delays . . . Rick, how can we thank you for interrupting your vacation and pinch-hitting right at the end? Thank goodness you and Bert had worked on this together so you knew what was happening."

"Don't worry about it," Rick assured her as an image of Isabelle flashed across his mind. "So, do you think you're going to be able to convince Bert to hire someone else to repair your roof?"

"It's being done even as we speak. I'm lucky the old fool didn't kill himself when he fell off that thing."

"You'll see he gets this briefcase and tell him the big news?"

"Absolutely."

"I know Marilee Jot plans on dropping by later and sneaking in a bottle of cheap champagne."

"His favorite kind. And, Rick, thanks

again. You're a lifesaver."

"No problem," he said, but as he retraced his way through the hospital, he mulled over what this little interlude had cost him. His father was disappointed in him — again — and Isabelle wouldn't even answer her phone.

He was used to his father's judgmental behavior. The old man had never valued a thing Rick really cared about except Isabelle. Rick knew his dad would never change and had come to peace with it during the past few weeks. He'd drive back to Seaport tonight, and the old man would huff and puff. Tomorrow, Rick planned to modify the folding chart table for the little yacht. All would be forgiven until Rick went back to his life and then it would start over again.

That's the way it worked with his dad.

But Isabelle?

As he slid behind the wheel, he had to admit that her reaction to him leaving for Portland had irritated the living daylights out of him. He'd tried to explain the nature of this emergency to her, but she hadn't listened. She'd been so busy jumping to conclusions, he'd decided to let her stew in her own juices. Damn if he would explain himself to her if she was going to act so unreasonable.

Her reaction played into his worst fear: that the lifestyle of the last few weeks — so reminiscent of times past — contributed to her growing feelings for him. That night on the beach when he'd confessed how he still felt about her and then tried to make her understand that the boat-building persona wasn't the real him and it never would be, she'd tuned him out. She'd been too wrapped up in reinventing the wheel to see that their future depended on building a whole new wheel.

At this point, he honestly didn't know if there was hope for the two of them. He only knew that he wasn't going to marry a woman who didn't support him, who didn't trust him, who couldn't see or love him for who he really was and not for who she so desperately wanted him to be.

The way he saw her. He knew Isabelle's faults and shortcomings the same way he knew her strengths and passions. If he could love her for everything she was as well as everything she wasn't, she should be able to do the same for him.

He was anxious to get back to the coast and see her. Anxious to know if they were on the verge of a beginning or the beginning of an end.

■ ■ ■ ■

Mrs. Pughill was back. She'd collected her stack of horoscopes. *(Day Eighteen: Open your heart to new responsibilities. Let a little sunshine into your life. Five stars.)* Isabelle had kept the kitten out of sight; no use getting the landlady in a tizzy over another pet. Thankfully, Mrs. Pughill hadn't said a word about the new carpet.

Not that Isabelle spent a lot of time worrying about Mrs. Pughill. Rick's father had called as the landlady left. Rick was on his way back to Seaport. All she could think about was the fact that she had to get out of town. Thus she had dug all her camping gear out of the closet and packed it into her trunk.

She'd let Rick down big-time. Her search at the library and on the Internet at home had flushed out the details of Bert Chesterfield and the Holgate case and now she recalled why the name sounded familiar.

Isabelle had spent her summers working at a summer school that Marilee Jot, an advocate for disabled youth, had founded near Seaport. While the school had been modest, the strides the kids made while having fun had been heartwarming.

Scoot ahead a couple of years to Isabelle's first classroom. One of the mother volunteers had a second child at home, a little girl with cerebral palsy. This woman was a tireless activist for her daughter. Isabelle could still recall the mother's excitement when she learned of Henrietta Holgate's bequest to Marilee Jot's nonprofit association: hundreds of acres of wooded forest bordering the ocean south of Seaport. The woman had gushed as she related plans for a wonderful complex where health professionals, family members and disabled children alike could participate in carefully structured play. She'd spoken of therapy dressed up like horseback riding and swimming; trails and lakes; beaches on which to spin lazy dreams — the hopes for this place had seemed endless. Then the lawsuits started.

Isabelle had discovered on the Portland newspaper's Web site that the day before the closing arguments in the preliminary trial were to be delivered, Marilee Jot's lawyer, Bert Chesterfield, had slid off his roof while replacing a few shingles.

Obviously, Rick had been filling in for Chesterfield and that's why he'd had to hurry back to Portland. The morning newspaper reported that the case had been thrown out of court. Rick wasn't mentioned by name but it was obvious that he'd been instrumental in taking Marilee Jot's dream one step closer to reality.

And that's why Isabelle didn't have the guts to face Rick again.

He'd tried to explain; she'd shut him out. Instead of compassion or curiosity or keeping an open mind, she'd reacted with suspicion and fear. When he'd tried to explain what was happening, she'd accused him of leaving his father in the lurch.

Now she faced the truth: it wasn't his dad or his dad's unfinished boat that had caused her knee-jerk reaction. The less noble truth was that it had felt as though he was leaving her, as though he might never come back . . . to her. He'd said they needed to talk about what they'd said to one another the night before he left. How could she bear to hear him tell her she'd moved too fast for him or worse, that he'd changed his mind altogether?

She packed Marnie's leash and dog food and then glanced around the kitchen for a last-minute inspection and spied a small orange bundle of fur asleep in her box.

The kitten! She'd forgotten about the kitten! She couldn't leave the poor little thing here all alone. Isabelle scanned the phone book and called the shelter. They told her to bring the kitten in, they'd find a home for her one way or another. Isabelle gathered the kitten food, then found a nice sturdy box with a lid and lined it with a clean towel for transportation.

But now, of course, the kitten was gone! A thorough search of the duplex turned up nothing. When half an hour had passed and the kitten still didn't appear, Isabelle gave up. She'd have to ask Mrs. Pughill for help. The landlady could use her key to access Isabelle's duplex to feed the little rascal while Isabelle was gone.

She knocked on Mrs. Pughill's door. Marnie, for once, stood off a little as though not wanting to get too close.

Mrs. Pughill took a few moments to answer, and when she did, she was holding beneath her double chin a small bundle of orange fur that clashed wildly with the remaining red hairs on the landlady's head. A gray fuzz was growing back however, leaving the possibilities for future hair color wide open.

How did the kitten get into Mrs. Pughill's apartment? Was there a hole in the wall? Surprised at this turn of events, Isabelle said, "Oh, my!"

"Isn't she adorable?" Mrs. Pughill gushed.

"I don't mind telling you I've been a little down since getting home from my sister's house. Those puppies were so darling! And foggy days are just flat-out depressing, don't you think?

"I —"

"Then I heard a scratching on my back door. I was sure a raccoon was out there, but I opened it to find this little sweetheart. I don't know where she could have come from! Her back and neck were damp, as though she'd been mauled!"

Isabelle felt like scratching her head. How did that tiny wisp of orange fur get all the way over to Mrs. Pughill's back door? She glanced at Marnie — no, that was impossible.

Meanwhile, Ignatz growled.

Glaring at her dog, Mrs. Pughill snapped, "Mind your manners, Ignatz! This little lamb is ours to take care of now. She can sleep in your bed with you." Turning back to Isabelle, she added, "It's like Madame Hortense said: 'Open your heart to new responsibilities. Let a little sunshine into your life.' And five stars, too! This little orange kitty is like a ray of sunshine, and that's just what I'm going to name her! It's destiny! That woman is a genius!"

Ignatz whined as though he'd been kicked.

The kitten mewed appealingly as she gazed at Isabelle with her gray eyes.

Isabelle smiled for the first time in three days.

Mrs. Pughill caught sight of Marnie and regained her old demeanor just like that! Glaring now at Isabelle, she said, "You just keep your beast away from little Sunshine, and that's a warning."

"Nice to have you back," Isabelle said dryly.

The relief at having the kitten in a good home (there wasn't a doubt in Isabelle's mind that Mrs. Pughill would devote herself to Sunshine; it was poor Ignatz who would get short shrifted now) faded away as Isabelle left Seaport behind. She'd camp her way south for the next week, then figure out a way to apologize to Rick. Right now she was too ashamed of herself, too embarrassed about the way she'd acted, too afraid of what he'd say. She was running away and she knew it.

Boy, it's just like they say: revenge is sweet and best served cold!

It was almost too easy. As soon as Isabelle read today's horoscope out loud, I knew what I was going to do. And when she started making plans to leave town, I knew I had to act fast. As soon as she got on the phone with the shelter, I grabbed little orange kitty by the scruff of her neck, wiggled through my dog door, jumped the fence, scratched Ignatz' door, dropped the kitten and hightailed it home.

And old Mrs. Pughill loved her! Five stars' worth!

Take that, Ignatz!

After several minutes of profound contentment, it dawned on me that Isabelle hadn't been talking much the past two or three days. I knew she was unhappy, I knew she'd gotten a phone call from Rick's dad, but I wasn't sure why we were suddenly going camping.

Were we meeting Rick?

Given the sadness in her eyes, I doubted it.

What had I missed?

Chapter Thirteen

Isabelle lay awake in her tent. It was raining so hard, who could sleep? Marnie lay beside her, both of them shivering every time the lightning and thunder came together.

"If we live through this night," Isabelle said as she ran her hand through Marnie's damp fur, "we'll go home, I promise. Rick should . . . well, it's time to go home."

Marnie made a little grumbling noise low in her throat. Isabelle took this as agreement.

They'd been gone for almost a week now. The state parks had been full, so Isabelle had pitched her tent in smaller camps with fewer amenities and thus fewer campers. As she spent most every day walking, and it didn't much matter to her if it was on a beach, a trail or an old dirt road, the smaller camps were fine.

But it had been raining for the past twenty-four hours and she and Marnie were both tired, dirty and wet. She was ready to go home and make some changes in her life. For instance, she was going to sign up for a cooking class; it was ridiculous for an almost-twenty-six-year-old woman not to know how to cook. A week of canned soup and chili had highlighted her inadequacies in this department.

And most importantly, she was going to give Rick what she owed him: an apology.

And then they could start over.

Maybe. . . .

"I know you mean this," Rick said two days later. Rick's dad had met his deadline, the lovely little ship had been paid for, launched and christened the *Windsong.* The new owner was thrilled to death and added a bonus. Isabelle had missed all of this, of course.

Now Rick was in his dad's guest room, busily stuffing his overnight bag with jeans and T-shirts. "I know you mean this from the bottom of your heart," he repeated, sparing her a glance from over his shoulder.

"Yes," Isabelle said firmly. "I do." She pulled on his arm to make him stop packing. "Rick, listen to me —"

"You left," he said, staring down at her hand which she withdrew. "You got mad at me and just ran off."

"No," she protested. "It wasn't like that. I'm sorry. I think I understand —"

"It's kind of late for that, Isabelle."

"You're disappointed in me," she whispered.

He turned again. Mouth in a straight line, eyes hard, he said, "How does it feel to have someone you love disappointed in you?"

"Awful," she answered truthfully. "Terrible."

With a sigh, he sat down on the bed and took her hands in his, pulling her close, wrapping his arms around her torso and laying his head against her chest. Isabelle felt tears burn behind her nose.

Tentatively, she touched his hair.

He looked up at her and for the first time she could ever recall, there were tears in his eyes.

Fear was beginning to tighten the muscles in her throat. "I'm sorry," she said again. "I should have trusted you. I should have believed in you. I know now what you were doing. It was noble. I just —"

He stood up then and looked down at her, smoothing the hair away from her face with trembling hands. The misery she saw on his face not only reflected the misery she felt in her own heart, but portended more misery to come.

"I got involved in this case when I interned with Bert. I got involved because I recognized Marilee Jot's name, I remembered that you spent your summers working with her. I see now it was a way for me to stay connected to you, Isabelle, even though we were no longer together."

"Rick. I —"

He kissed her forehead. "I love you," he said. "I think I'll always love you. I don't want to hurt you. But I'm not the man you want in your heart of hearts, and I can't spend the rest of my life like that. I grew up not being enough. I can't make a future of it, too."

"But if you love me and I love you —"

He put a finger over her lips. "You know I'm right. We keep saying it over and over, but it's true. Love isn't always enough."

He ruffled Marnie's ears, said, "Bye, lamb chop," picked up his duffel bag, and walked toward the door.

How could he walk away without giving her another chance? Surely he would turn around . . . He disappeared through the door as she sat there dithering with herself. She heard his footsteps on the stairs and the distant slam of a door.

Isabelle buried her head in her hands.

Marnie licked her leg and whined.

Isabelle took me home that night and after wandering around in a daze for a while, went to bed, so distracted she forgot to turn out the kitchen lights after she fed me or even latch the dog door!

I stared at that door for a long time, knowing exactly what I had to do but putting it off. I'd just been camping and it was good to be home!

But my dreams of a united family were over unless I took the matter into my own hands . . . er, paws.

So, in true wire fox terrier character, I put my chin up, took a final look around the apartment and jumped through the dog door.

As I hopped over the fence, I hoped I'd see Isabelle again someday. The poor girl needed me and I hated the thought of causing her more pain, but sometimes a dog's got to do what a dog's got to do.

Isabelle woke up the next morning with no interest in doing anything. There were just a couple of weeks before school began again, a prospect that ordinarily thrilled her but this year left her unmoved.

Good thing she had a little while to conjure up some enthusiasm before the kids filled the classroom, she thought, and decided that perhaps going to the school and getting a head start on the bulletin boards would help fill the void in her heart.

"Marnie?" she called after brushing her teeth and pulling on shorts and a blouse, listening for the jangle of dog tags.

She walked out to the kitchen, expecting to see her dog camped out by her food dish, but the room was empty. That's when she noticed the latch undone on the dog door.

"Oh, brother, if she's jumped that fence again . . ." Isabelle muttered, opening the back door and looking out into the backyard.

No dog.

She went through the house to the front door and swung that open.

"Marnie?"

Alarmed, Isabelle grabbed the leash and shut the door behind her. She knocked on Mrs. Pughill's door, wincing when she heard Ignatz howl at the intrusion. She heard Mrs. Pughill's voice raised over the barking. "No, Ignatz! You're scaring little Sunshine!"

Mrs. Pughill finally flung open the door, wearing her dowdy brown bathrobe and no socks. Ignatz lurked near her ankles as always, though there was an aura of confusion about the watery-eyed poodle that was new.

"I heard you calling for your mutt," Mrs. Pughill said. Looking a tad smug, Sunshine peeked out of the landlady's roomy pocket.

"She's wandered off. Have you seen her?"

"Check my roses. She loves to dig them up."

They both looked out at the rose garden.

"If you see her, will you let her in my apartment? I'm going to walk around the neighborhood and see if I can find her."

"I don't have time —"

"Mrs. Pughill. Make time, please." And with that, Isabelle turned around and walked stiffly down the driveway. She walked the streets surrounding her house, calling Marnie's name, circling the blocks on either side of the duplex before returning home to see if the dog had doubled back. Then she got her keys and drove to Rick's dad's boatyard, where she found the old man in his shop, which seemed enormous without the sailboat in residence.

"Have you seen Marnie?" she asked.

Carl Manning looked up from his workbench where he was servicing some of his tools. He had limited use of his injured hand now. He said, "No. Should I have?"

"No," she said. "I just can't find her. I

thought maybe she came here looking for Rick —"

"As you well know," Carl Manning snapped, "Rick has gone back to his fancy life in the city."

Taking a deep breath, Isabelle put into words the thoughts that had been rambling around in her head for days. She said, "Rick is a wonderful man, Carl. He loves what he does. And what he does is important. You should be proud of him."

Carl turned to face her. He looked stunned by her defense of his son. He said, "He sold out for money."

"No," she said. "He chose not to sell out to get your or my approval. He's strong, he's full of conviction. He's following his heart, just like you did when you chose your career path. It would be like someone being mad at you all the time because you wanted to build sailboats and not raise . . . I don't know . . . turkeys."

"But —"

"Same thing," she said. "I hope you think about what I've said. I think it's too late for me, but you're his father, there's still time for you."

Carl shook his head.

Isabelle said, "I have to go find Marnie. She's not the smartest dog in the world when it comes to traffic. If she shows up here, call and leave a message on my machine, okay?"

Isabelle drove back to the duplex, then started circling the neighborhood. As the hours passed and Marnie didn't show up, she began to feel as though she'd never see her dog again. It seemed as if she'd disappeared off the face of the earth.

By afternoon, she'd stopped driving and started making posters with Marnie's picture featured front and center. By evening, she was plastering every electricity and telephone pole with the posters, offering a reward, doing everything she could think of to keep her spirits up and her thoughts positive.

How she longed to call Rick.

A couple of months before, she would never have dreamed that Marnie would run away like this, but the little dog had been acting strange now for weeks. She'd torn up carpet and tissue boxes, escaped yards and bedrooms. She'd played hide-and-seek with Chloe's picture, stowed away in Carl's truck, apparently speed-dialed Rick and who knew what else. The point was, there was no telling what she'd do next!

When the phone rang, Isabelle answered

it on the first ring.

"It's me," Heather said. "Just want to catch up on things. We're trying to decide if we want to learn the sex of our baby when I have my sonogram in a few weeks. John says we should go for it. I'm not certain. What would you do, Isabelle?"

This dilemma seemed as foreign to Isabelle as someone asking her opinion on how to properly construct an igloo. Without Rick, would there ever be love, and without love, would there ever be marriage and a baby of her own? Begging off in order to keep the line open in case someone called about Marnie, Isabelle sat in a stupor until the phone rang again.

This call was from a child who had found a dog the week before. The next call was Rick's dad wanting a progress report, then one from a woman who had lost her German shepherd and wanted Isabelle to keep an eye out for him while she looked for Marnie.

The apartment seemed empty without Marnie. The poor little thing was probably starved and alone. At least she was wearing her tags. The dog license was traceable to Isabelle and the lilac heart was engraved with Marnie's name and Isabelle's phone number.

When it started raining, Isabelle felt a chasm open in her heart.

The call Isabelle had been waiting for didn't come until nine o'clock, just as it was getting dark. "I've got your dog," a man's voice said. "My boy offered her a doughnut and caught her. Is there a reward?"

"Absolutely," Isabelle said, stunned by the call. She realized then that she'd not allowed herself to hope for a happy resolution. "Is she okay? Where are you calling from?"

"She's okay. A little tired maybe, that's all. Billy tied her up outside when he came home to watch television. We live twenty miles upriver from Astoria."

For a second, Isabelle said nothing. How in the world had Marnie traveled almost thirty miles away from home? Had someone stolen her? Had *this* man taken her and was he now concocting a story in order to exact what amounted to a ransom?

She didn't care, she realized; all she wanted was Marnie back home where she belonged. She said, "I'll be there in less than an hour."

"Nah," he said around a yawn. "I've been up felling trees since before dawn. I'm doing work down your way tomorrow, I'll bring her to you."

"I don't mind —"

"I'll have her at your place before seven," he said firmly.

Reluctantly, Isabelle agreed. She couldn't *make* the man give her his exact address or stay awake until she got there.

The euphoria at finding Marnie was hard to contain. It was too late to call Carl Manning and Mrs. Pughill wouldn't care. Isabelle drifted around the duplex for several moments, grinning ear to ear before finally falling into bed.

She'd assumed she'd sleep the sleep of the dead after so many nights of wakefulness, but she was wrong. She felt unsettled and uneasy. Marnie might be as good as home, but she wasn't actually home.

And then there was Rick, an ache in her heart she suspected might never go away. When she closed her eyes, she could almost feel his arms around her. How could a love like theirs be over? Again. How could she have let this happen?

Again.

She sucked up the tears and shook her head. If he didn't love her enough to fight for her — for them — well, she would forget him. She would cast his memory away forever. She'd done it once; by gum, she would do it again! She had her pride, and this time she'd wrap it around herself like a big heavy coat on a frosty day. It would protect her, it would keep her safe.

By the middle of the night, she'd given up on sleep. At daybreak she was mopping the kitchen floor when the phone rang.

"Sorry," the gruff voice from the night before said. "I heard some barking during the middle of the night. We get raccoons and opossums — I figure your dog got all riled up. Anyway, it looks like she chewed through her rope. Guess she took off."

"You left her tied up outside all night?" Isabelle cried. "With wild animals prowling about?"

"She seemed okay," he said.

"But it was raining —"

"She scooted under the truck to stay dry," he said, his voice growing less apologetic and more defensive by the moment.

"Please, tell me where you live," she said. "Give me some place to start looking."

He snapped out a reply and hung up.

Isabelle replaced the receiver. The phone rang again almost at once. This time it was Rick's dad wanting a progress report, which Isabelle gave him without breaking into tears — no small feat.

She sat there for a moment, longing to call Rick, but she kept hearing his pronouncement that they were over, kept seeing his back as he exited the door.

Grabbing her car keys and a pile of posters, she headed out for the last place anyone had seen Marnie.

The town where Marnie had spent most of the previous night turned out to be little more than a wide spot in the road, one of those places where five or six houses and three times as many cars are clustered together within throwing distance of the highway. Nevertheless, Isabelle plastered every pole or flat surface with posters, then she knocked on doors. There weren't many people home on a Tuesday morning.

She did find the address the man on the phone had given her and, in the muddy yard, a skinny boy of about ten next to the rear end of an old truck up on blocks.

"Are you Billy?" she asked.

He nodded.

Her gaze drifted down to the chewed off string still tied to the bumper. It was hard to imagine Marnie tied up like that all night. She said, "You found my dog."

He grinned. "She wanted some of my doughnut so I gave her a bite."

"Doughnuts just happen to be her favorite food," Isabelle said, opening her wallet and extracting a few bills. "Will you see that your dad gets this to pay for the long distance calls? Maybe there'll be enough left over to buy you some more doughnuts."

"She was a neat dog," Billy said, pocketing the cash.

It sounded too much like an epitaph to Isabelle who drove home where she checked the message machine — no calls — and then stared at the phone.

Once again, she burned with the desire to call Rick.

Once again, she didn't.

Twelve more hours passed before the phone rang again. This time, it was a woman who called. She explained she had seen Marnie hours before but hadn't been able to phone until now as she and her husband had been out biking and had just pedaled home.

"Brett and I saw her a little east of Riverview," the woman said. "We were eating our lunch down near the water when this scroungy-looking dog suddenly appeared. There was a piece of twine or something tied to her collar, so we figured she was lost. While I fed her bits of cheese, Brett tried to catch her, but she escaped by wiggling out of her collar. We heard her yelp as she ran off and when we chased after her, we found blood on the ground, but the dog just vanished! Do you want me to send you her tags?"

This time when Isabelle replaced the receiver, she sat there for a moment staring into space. Without her tags, Marnie was just another stray with no way to be linked back to Isabelle. Apparently, she was wounded. She could be . . .

No, she wouldn't allow herself to think the worst.

She dashed out to her car and retrieved the map of Oregon she kept in the glove box. She brought it back inside and spread it open on the kitchen table, and with a marker, drew a circle around the town in which Marnie had spent the first night, then another circle around Riverview, a city about thirty miles east of the first town.

The conclusion she reached was preposterous! And yet . . .

The phone rang again.

"Is she home? Have you found her?"

It was Rick. Isabelle managed to mumble, "No."

"Why didn't you call me?" he demanded. "I had to get this news from my dad."

"Why didn't I call you?" she repeated. "Why do you think I didn't call you?"

His voice lost some of its edge. "I'm

sorry," he said. "I'm worried. Why in the world would she run away from you? She loves you."

"She loves you, too," Isabelle said, and then gave voice to her newly drawn suspicion. "Crazy as this sounds, I think she's working her way to Portland. To you."

There was stunned silence on his end of the phone as Isabelle related the last two calls and the devastating news that Marnie was now hurt in some way and without identification.

"I can't sit here not knowing," she said at last. "Without her tags, I'll never even know if she's been hit by a car or —"

"Stop," Rick said. "You said you made posters. Did you use your computer?"

"Yes. I —"

"E-mail me what you have. I'll print out a bunch. Tomorrow morning, I'll start at my end and you start at Riverview. We'll put up the posters as we drive toward each other. It's not that busy a road, especially at your end. We'll meet somewhere in the middle and compare notes. Maybe we'll find her trotting along the wayside."

"Do you think there's a chance?" Isabelle asked, feeling a surge of hope.

"There's always a chance, isn't there?"

How she longed to agree, but she knew

her voice would reflect that it wasn't just Marnie's safety she was talking about, it was also their relationship. She came close to telling him no thanks, that Marnie was her dog and she'd find her on her own, thank you very much.

But the truth was she needed all the help she could get. The truth was she ached to see Rick, to hold him. There'd be time for her pride later.

CHAPTER FOURTEEN

I'd always known the weak spot of my plan was the necessity of letting people close enough to read my tags so they could then report my whereabouts to Isabelle.

That and the no breakfast, no lunch, no dinner thing. Oh, and the paws. Mine ached.

Still, no risk, no gain, or something like that, so I was careful of the people I chose. The kid with the doughnut, for instance. Who knew he had a string in his pocket? And take those people on their bikes. That's why I chose them. I'm not exactly built for bike riding. I thought for sure they'd have a cell phone, but no, I managed to find the only thirty-something people in the world without one.

When the man made a lunge for me, I'm afraid it awakened something primal in my soul. Forgetting that I was depending on humans to report my whereabouts to Isabelle, I growled and snapped as he pinned me to the ground. Then he made the mistake of grabbing my collar. With a twist, I was free, dashing through the dense brush and berry vines where no human could follow, exhilarated and frightened at the same time until a sharp pain in my right paw stopped me. I'd found a shard of glass and it was jammed right up there between my pads. Ouch!

Limping now, I wormed my way under a bush and tried to collect my thoughts. It was then I noticed I no longer jingled-jangled when I moved. My collar and tags were gone! I felt naked without them! Lost! Scared!

These feelings just got worse when I finally found the main highway. The last few minutes had been such a jumble; I was turned around and thoroughly disoriented. I wasn't entirely sure which way was which . . .

There was a thicket beside the road that would provide good cover for the night. It was cool in there and I was free to lick my paw and concentrate. You haven't forgotten I'm psychic, have you?

Not that it seemed to be doing me a lot of good.

Isabelle drove slowly, stopping often to ask everyone she saw if they'd seen Marnie, leaving an avalanche of posters in her wake. She stopped at picnic waysides and fishing ramps, calling Marnie's name over and over again until her throat was raw. She asked people at vegetable stands and flower kiosks, motels and gas stations. Had anyone seen this dog?

No one had.

Ten miles upriver from the spot where the picnickers had attempted to capture Marnie the day before, Isabelle pulled off the road. She chose a grassy spot shaded by massive oak trees in which to park. She suddenly had the odd sensation that she'd gone too far — that Marnie was somewhere behind her, hurt, hiding maybe.

She needed to turn around and go back; she knew this as much as she knew anything. She also felt a sense of dread that came over her like a chill, a premonition of sorts that Marnie was beyond help.

Should she go back and risk missing Rick? What if he'd found Marnie further up the road? It had been almost twenty-four hours since the cyclists had seen Marnie; she could easily be another ten or twenty miles closer to Portland.

What if this premonition of doom that had settled over Isabelle's heart was just that and nothing more?

Should she stay right here in the wide spot and wait for Rick to meet her? A glance at her watch showed her that he should reach this spot within the hour, maybe sooner depending on when he'd left that morning.

Or should she proceed as they planned and keep driving toward Portland, turning back only after she met Rick?

Torn by indecision, she felt a sense of bleakness she'd seldom felt in her life; a sense that she'd lost everything and everyone who mattered to her and that somehow, it was all her fault.

She got out of the car and leaned back against the front fender, arms folded across her chest, eyes closed as dappled sunlight fought its way through the heavy boughs of the tree looming above and played across her face.

"Snap out of it!" she admonished herself. "Marnie needs you." Her next thought was of Rick. Thanks to Isabelle, he now believed Marnie was on her way to find him. Who knew if that was correct? If Marnie was lost forever, how would Rick feel thinking he was somehow the cause? Terrible, that's how.

She shouldn't have involved him.

He involved himself, she reminded herself. *He called you. He cares. He loves her.*

And in that moment when all seemed lost, she also realized something else with blinding certainty: *Rick loves you, too. And not in that "love is not enough" way he talked about.*

He said it was too late; he was wrong. She'd been selfish and immature for far too long, and she wasn't going to compound it now by letting her pride stand in the way of getting him back. Rick was her man the same way she was his woman. That had been the truth years before and it was the truth now. It would always be the truth.

Some of the hopelessness left her and she took a deep breath. She would drive back the way she'd come. Marnie was back there, she just knew it.

Within a mile, she began second-guessing her plan. After five miles, she was ready to turn around again. It took her another mile to find a suitable spot in which to turn, and as she slowed, she saw a movement in the bushes on the opposite side of the road that sent her heart into her throat.

Could it be Marnie? A sudden influx of cars whizzed past as she fought to look over and around them, hoping it was her dog and not just a wild animal, and hoping that if it was Marnie that she wouldn't dash out into the road.

The traffic finally died down enough for Isabelle to make a U-turn and pull to a stop. As she climbed out of her car, she kept her eyes on the bushes she'd seen move.

"Marnie!" she called, walking briskly though the deep grass. "Marnie!"

A small, bedraggled shape limped from the thicket.

"Marnie!" Isabelle cried.

The dog looked up. For a second, as their gazes connected, neither one of them moved, and then Marnie bounded over the rough terrain separating them, springing up into Isabelle's arms, injury seemingly forgotten, landing with such momentum that it sent Isabelle reeling backward until she hit her own car with a thump. She wrapped her arms around her filthy dog, never so happy to see anyone or anything in her life.

Marnie whined and cried. She barked and quivered. Isabelle felt warm tears slide down her cheeks as she kissed the dog's furry head and held her trembling pet close to her heart.

They both seemed to hear a car arriving at the same moment, for they both looked up as Rick swerved across the road and parked his car nose to nose with Isabelle's. He was out in a blink, his arms wrapped around the two of them in two blinks, his face reflecting the relief and wonder Isabelle felt flowering in her chest.

And Isabelle realized her world was complete right there in that moment and she wished it would never change.

"She's hurt," he said finally, touching Marnie's blood-stained paw.

They examined her foot before Rick insisted she be put in his car with its leather upholstery, thereby sparing the fabric in Isabelle's car. Isabelle was glad he'd put the top down for the drive; she could barely take her eyes from Marnie, she could still barely believe she'd found her, that she'd been drawn to the exact spot where Marnie waited.

What a miracle.

Marnie stretched out on the back seat, panting with relief or joy or fatigue — who could tell?

Eventually, Isabelle, staring at the grass, whispered, "I can't let you go, Rick. I'll turn into a stalker if I have to, but I love you and I'm not going to disappear quietly again. I want you to be a lawyer, the best lawyer in the world. Or a brick layer. Or a ditch digger or a judge. I'll support anything you do, just let me love you."

She felt Rick's fingers graze her skin as he lifted her chin and stared down at her. "My dad told me what you said to him," he said at last.

"I meant every word."

She waited with suspended breath, unable

to read the look in his dark eyes. Finally, he addressed Marnie. "What do you think, lamb chop? Do you think a boy and a girl and a cat and a dog can be happy living together? Do you think there's a chance for us?"

Marnie woofed with authority.

Rick looked at Isabelle. "You know her best, what do you think that bark meant?"

"I think it means she wants us together," Isabelle whispered.

"So do I," Rick said softly, leaning closer until their lips touched with a jolt that set them both back on their heels, and then just as quickly, propelled them back into each other's arms.

He kissed her face a hundred times as he pulled her close. "My love, my darling," he whispered against her ear. "Say you'll marry me tomorrow."

She held herself away and gazed up into his eyes. "I'll marry you tomorrow," she said.

Marnie woofed again as they kissed.

Of course I got scolded for running off, but I never take that kind of thing seriously. I took the visit to the vet and the subsequent stitches in my foot very seriously, however, as I had to wear an inverted flowerpot around my neck for the next three weeks.

Oh, the indignity of it.

And if you don't think old Stealth Cat didn't gloat, then you haven't been paying attention.

After the wedding (you figured on a wedding, didn't you?) Isabelle and I moved into Rick's apartment, though I'm using my psychic abilities to coerce our way back to Seaport. Isabelle got a job teaching city kids, so Stealth Cat and I spend a lot of time together. He's not so bad, but don't tell him I said that.

We're all looking for a larger place now, one with an extra bedroom because Isabelle is expecting a baby. I figure if I can handle having a cat making goo-goo eyes at me all the time, I can handle a baby.

Right?

ABOUT THE AUTHOR

Alice Sharpe met her husband-to-be on a cold, foggy beach in Northern California. One year later they were married. Their union has survived the rearing of two children, a handful of earthquakes registering over 6.5, numerous cats and a few special dogs, the latest of which is a yellow Lab named Annie Rose. Alice and her husband now live in a small rural town in Oregon, where she devotes the majority of her time to pursuing her second love, writing.

Alice loves to hear from readers. You can write her at P.O. Box 755, Brownsville, OR 97327. SASE for reply is appreciated. Or visit her Web site at www.alicesharpe.com.